Will   Irma   Taranee   Cornelia   Hay Lin

Worlds Apart

Adapted by **KATE EGAN**

an imprint of
HYPERION BOOKS FOR CHILDREN
New York

© 2005 Disney Enterprises, Inc.

W.I.T.C.H. Will Irma Taranee Cornelia Hay Lin is a trademark of Disney Enterprises, Inc.
Volo® is a registered trademark of Disney Enterprises, Inc.
Volo/Hyperion Books for Children are imprints of Disney Children's Book Group, L.L.C.

Printed in the United States of America
First Edition
1 3 5 7 9 10 8 6 4 2

This book is set in 12/16.5 Hiroshige Book.
ISBN 0-7868-5192-9
Visit www.clubwitch.com

ONE

In Candracar, Luba, one of the Elders of the Congregation and the Keeper of the Aurameres, stalked out of the majestic Aura Hall. Her long robes swished around her ankles as she frantically searched for the Oracle. When she brought his attention to what she had just seen, there would be no denying his great mistake. The Oracle would be forced to admit that he'd been wrong about the girls from Heatherfield who were now the Guardians. There could be no question.

Luba had always had her doubts about the five girls who had been anointed by the Oracle as Guardians of the Veil. They were supposed to defend and protect the barrier between dark, troubled Metamoor and the earth.

And, miraculously, they had managed to save the troubled world—even Luba could not deny their successes. They had conquered the evil Prince Phobos and returned the rightful heir to the throne. The young Elyon had now joined the long line of queens who ruled over Meridian, the city within Metamoor.

But Will, Irma, Taranee, Hay Lin, and Cornelia were only girls, after all, and sometimes they made mistakes—costly mistakes. Luba couldn't see why the Oracle put up with such nonsense. While the Guardians' powers were impressive and significant, the girls had gotten themselves into quite a lot of trouble. Controlling water, earth, air, fire, and energy proved to be most helpful as the girls battled the evildoers in Metamoor, but what about how they all treated each other? Recently, the girls' bickering had been not helpful. No, not helpful at all.

Picking up her pace, Luba made her way through the magnificent Temple of Candracar, the vast and mysterious place at the very center of infinity. From the Temple, the great and all-knowing Oracle observed the world. Advised by the Council of Elders, he intervened only when he had to. Luba hoped—no, *expected*—that this would be one of those times.

More than anybody, the Oracle should have known that the girls' work had only just begun, and that the repair of the Veil and the twelve portals was just a part of their task. Everything they did was important to the task of maintaining balance and peace. There was no room for costly errors.

While Luba was a member of the Oracle's Council, she had another job, too: to observe and protect the Aurameres, the five spheres of magical essence that represented the Guardians' powers. They spun around and around in the towering Aura Hall, shining with their energy. The hall was protected by invisible forces—but even those forces were powerless against the changes that had just occurred.

Once, the Aurameres had been so large that they occupied the entire room; now they were only the size of Luba's hand! And if the Aurameres were smaller, it meant the girls' powers had been reduced, too. It was just as Luba had always suspected: the girls couldn't handle their powers. They couldn't manage to stick together and to act as a group. They simply didn't have what it took to be Guardians of the Veil.

Finally, Luba found the Oracle. He hovered above a platform at the very center of the Temple. The walls around him were covered with elaborate carvings, making the space a very ethereal and beautiful one. The Oracle's eyes were closed, his breathing was deep, and Luba knew he would not have wanted to be interrupted. But she interrupted him anyway.

"The Aurameres have dwindled!" Luba whispered urgently.

The Oracle snapped out of his meditation and without hesitation followed her silently to the Aura Hall. She knew that her declaration would force him to take action.

She gestured at the floating spheres, shadows of their former selves. "Look at them!" she spat. "I find the situation alarming!"

The Oracle calmly nodded. "I see them, Luba. And I'm listening."

Was there a hint of impatience in his voice? Luba wondered. She watched cautiously as the Oracle approached the Aurameres and plucked them one by one out of the air. The spheres shone brilliantly in his hand.

"Before your eyes, Luba," the Oracle stated, "these Aurameres represent the Guardians' great powers."

Luba wouldn't have dared to defy the Oracle or to dishonor him in any way. But that's what she felt like doing now. Her blood was boiling. She knew what the orbs were for and what their light represented. She didn't need a review.

Then the Oracle sighed heavily. "But the eyes you use to observe, Luba, are not enough to truly see!" The all-knowing Oracle looked directly into Luba's feline face. "And the true power of the Chosen Ones cannot be measured."

Luba tried to control her temper. Couldn't the Oracle understand what was happening? He was supposed to see and know *everything*.

"There is a darkness clouding their friendship!" Luba cried. "And this is the result!"

One of these days, she thought, the Oracle was going to have to admit he'd made an error. With the Guardians' powers at such a low ebb, there was no telling what trouble the girls would stumble into.

The Oracle didn't respond, and Luba hoped that her words were sinking in. At that moment, Tibor decided to speak. Tibor was one of the Elders, too. Until then, he had been silent, thoughtfully stroking his long beard, which nearly touched the floor.

"They're young!" Tibor exclaimed. "They have a rebellious spirit!"

"They're weak, Tibor! I've said that from the start!" Luba replied. She tried to keep her feline features neutral, but somehow her voice still twisted into a snarl. Tibor *would* take the Oracle's side, Luba thought. He always did. But somebody had to speak the truth before it was too late.

Tibor's voice was that of an old man, slow and shaky. Yet somehow he still spoke with great authority. "You are unfair, Keeper of the Aurameres!" he boomed. "You yourself rejoiced when the Guardians defeated Prince Phobos!"

Luba had already conceded that the Guardians had performed their mission well. But many more dangers remained for the Guardians to face, and Tibor knew that as well as Luba did.

"It seems to be the only thing they've

managed to do in their Guardian roles!" she shot back. "Pure luck!" Surely one victory was not enough to prove anything, Luba thought.

"What impudence!" roared Tibor.

Luba knew that Tibor couldn't bear it when the Oracle's judgment was questioned. "When the Oracle spoke of powers that cannot be seen, he meant . . ."

Just then the Oracle grasped Tibor's elbow and led him out of the Aura Hall. "Come, Tibor!" he said. "Don't underestimate Luba! She understands! She knows!"

Luba relaxed for a moment. Could the Oracle have been listening to her after all? Her hopes were shattered, however, when she heard the Oracle's next words.

"What Luba does not know is that a test is being given!" he said in a soft whisper.

Luba could hardly believe her ears. Another test? she wondered. When would the Oracle stop testing the Guardians and acknowledge their failure?

"Bah!" she said quietly to herself. "He does nothing but put the earthlings through useless, senseless trials."

Luba took up her usual post in the hall. She

noticed that the Aurameres had shrunk even further since the Oracle had left the room. Before much longer she would be able to fit all five of them into the palm of one hand.

Not even the unhealthy appearance of the Aurameres has convinced the Oracle that our Guardians are unfit, Luba mused. So what could convince him?

At first Luba wasn't sure what more she could do. But if her fate—and the fate of the world—rested in the hands of these girls, well . . . Luba shuddered. It was too horrible to think about. They'd all be doomed.

Rolling up the sleeves of her robe, Luba exposed her muscular arms. They were furred, like a tiger's, and muscular as a tiger's, too. Luba's strong spirit came to life. "Someone has to open the Oracle's eyes! Before it's too late!" she said, determined.

Then she drew her hands together and began to weave magic in the air. "And that someone is me!" she cackled.

TWO

Irma trudged home from school with none of her usual spunk and energy. Usually she had one eye out for any hottie who might happen to glance her way. But today she stared at the ground as she walked, hands buried deep in her pockets. It had been a long day at school. A lonely one, too. Irma missed her four best friends.

Not long ago, Irma had been *this* close to Will, Taranee, Cornelia, and Hay Lin. Will and Taranee were both new in Heatherfield, the town where Irma had lived all her life, but that didn't matter. Just days after they'd arrived at the Sheffield Institute, Will and Taranee had been eating lunch with Irma, Hay Lin, and Cornelia. They'd even started hanging out together after school.

Irma would never forget the afternoon the five girls had spent at Hay Lin's apartment, above the Chinese restaurant her parents ran. Strange things had been happening. . . . They were almost impossible to describe, much less explain. And then Hay Lin's grandmother swept in to do just that! What she had to tell the girls was shocking.

It was no accident that Will had been seeing things and that Irma had made water obey her commands. A powerful magic had been inside each of them. And when the Oracle anointed them as Guardians, their powers, united, became stronger.

Now Taranee could summon fire to light up any darkness. She could communicate telepathically, too! Hay Lin's power was over air, so she could float on a breeze or conjure up a howling wind. With her power over earth, Cornelia could move mountains—or nurture any growing thing. And Irma herself had magical power over water, which meant that she could call up a low tide or a massive flood whenever she was in the mood.

Irma loved the way each girl's personality fit

her particular magic. Taranee could be quiet—except when she was heated up about something. Hay Lin floated through life, not taking anything very seriously. Solid Cornelia, on the other hand, was always practical, with her feet on the ground. And Irma's water-magic suited her just right, too. Irma liked to play it cool. People didn't usually see her sweat.

Only Will was sometimes uncomfortable with her magic. Will's was the strongest and the most mysterious of all. She linked her friends' powers together with the Heart of Candracar, a beautiful orb that "lived" deep inside of Will. When the Heart was ready to draw together the magic of the other four girls, it appeared in Will's palm—and then their powers became stronger.

Will's power made her the leader of the other girls—the initials of whose names spelled out W.I.T.C.H. But even though she had proven herself the unquestionable leader of the group, Will didn't love being in charge. It wasn't always easy, especially when she had big decisions to make.

Along with their powers, the girls had been given a mission. It didn't take a genius to figure out that the Guardians of the Veil, well, guarded the Veil. But it was pretty scary to find out that the Veil was in such bad shape—and that they were supposed to fix it!

Long ago, the Oracle had put the Veil in place to protect the earth from Metamoor and its greedy ruler, Prince Phobos. Phobos had already conquered his own world, subjecting all of its creatures to his dark rule. Metamoor's only light existed in its largest city, Meridian, hidden away deep in Phobos's splendid palace. The only hope belonged to the few flunkies Phobos kept close by him. But even absolute power wasn't enough for Phobos. He wanted to conquer the earth, too, transforming its beauty and its goodness.

The Veil had remained intact through the last millennium, even when fearsome creatures from Metamoor had tried to breach it. But cosmic forces had battered the Veil when the new millennium arrived. Suddenly it was weaker and more vulnerable than ever before, with twelve holes, or portals, opening directly between the two worlds. Soon, giant green reptiles and dangerous blue thugs began to slip through the portals. Some were intent on the earth's destruction, while some wanted to journey to the earth, hoping for a better fate than the one that awaited them back in Metamoor.

With their tremendous powers, the girls had managed to close the portals to Heatherfield. When they took Phobos to Candracar, the Oracle lifted the Veil, because it had become useless. And the Oracle finally sealed the portals for good. Prince Phobos was replaced with Princess Elyon. Peace was at hand. All was well with the world.

Right? Right, thought Irma. Then why aren't my friends at peace, too? The five girls had amazing powers. But none of them were able to travel back in time—which was what Irma wished she could do at that very moment.

She missed the way things had used to be.

Let's be honest, Irma admitted to herself. We're not a team anymore.

Now, Cornelia was holed up at home, watering the flower that was the great love of her life. Caleb, before Phobos got his hands on him, had been a total hottie. Now he was just a flower.

Adding to the drama was the news that Will's mom had requested a transfer from her company. She and Will would be moving to another city at the end of the year unless Will could figure out a way to change her mom's mind. Irma almost felt sorry for Will—before she remembered how mad she was at her.

Irma's temper flared when she remembered her last conversation with Will—if you could call it a conversation. She had a pretty good idea for fixing Will's problem. But Will wouldn't hear a word of her brilliant plan. She was always so particular about how the other girls used their magic.

So let her move away, Irma fumed. See if I care.

Kicking a stone across the sidewalk, Irma groaned as she continued to walk home. She was so lost in her thoughts that she didn't notice two figures standing in front of her very own house, leaning against a car. As she approached, one of them called out to her.

"Hi, Irma!"

Irma jumped.

"Agent Medina! Agent McTiennan!" Irma stammered like a fool. She'd met those two Interpol agents before. They worked with Irma's father, who was the police sergeant in

Heatherfield. The agents were specialists in the Missing Persons department and had been sent to Heatherfield after Elyon disappeared. "What brings you here?" Irma asked when she recovered from her shock.

"We're waiting for your father," Agent McTiennan said. "We're going to your friend Elyon's house."

Irma put on her best innocent expression and clasped her hands behind her back. "You aren't still investigating her disappearance, are you?"

Agent McTiennan chuckled. "You bet we are!"

Agent Medina didn't say a word. She just crossed her arms over her chest and glared at Irma through her large, round glasses.

Wonder what her problem is, Irma thought.

Irma was pretty sure the agents wouldn't find Elyon, considering that Elyon was now the queen of Metamoor. But there was no telling what they *might* stumble across if they searched Elyon's old house. Irma wouldn't have wanted anyone to find out the truth about her friends . . . even if she wasn't on speaking terms with any of them.

The truth about Elyon was that she'd once lived in Heatherfield, like any other girl who went to Sheffield Institute. She had been Cornelia's best friend, and together they had been the most popular girls in school, true Infielders, as the popular kids were called. That had all changed when the girls were given their powers. Elyon had unknowingly betrayed them to creatures from Meridian. Then, slowly, she had been won over to the dark side. It had turned out that Prince Phobos was her long-lost brother. And he had lied to her, in order to align her with him and his evil plans.

The Guardians couldn't stand by and do nothing while their friend became their enemy. Eventually they had helped Elyon see the evil in her brother—and then they had helped her lead an uprising against him. Now Elyon was back in Meridian, ruling the place where she was born. Her family was there with her, too, so her house in Heatherfield remained abandoned. The police didn't know what to make of it. And all Irma knew was this: at one time, there'd been a portal to Meridian in Elyon's basement. It was the first one she'd ever seen.

Irma fumbled for something to say to the

agents. Luckily, she was saved by her dad.

Sergeant Lair walked out of the house, slammed the front door shut, and bounded down the front steps. "Hi, guys!" he rumbled in his deep voice. Then he turned to his daughter and ruffled her hair. "Hi, Irma! Weren't you going to the pool with Will?"

Irma wondered if her dad had any clue as to how many products were in her hair right now. Ruffling could be hazardous to his health! She squirmed out of his reach and smoothed down her hair, trying to repair the damage. "We finished early," she explained.

"Lucky you!" her dad said, grinning. "Wish I could say the same. I have to wrap up a ton of work!" He turned back to Medina and McTiennan. "Speaking of which," he said, addressing the agents, "did they give you the files?"

"No," McTiennan replied. "The guys at Forensics are waiting for your signature."

"Gotcha!" said Sergeant Lair, nodding. He already had a plan. "Let's go to Elyon's first, and then down to headquarters." He clambered into the agents' unmarked car.

Irma waltzed over to the car. She knew that

she should let them go. But she just *had* to find out more. "Um, what's left to see at the house?" she asked, a little nervously.

Agent Medina stared so hard at Irma that she seemed to glue her to the sidewalk with a steady, laser glare.

"Detectives had the wall in the basement knocked down," Irma's dad answered. "Now we can get a look behind it and see if we can find any clues."

Irma's eyes bugged out as she gripped the open window between her and her dad. "What?" she asked, dumbfounded. The portal was right behind that wall. She did her best to backtrack when she felt Medina's eyes boring into her. "That is . . . I mean . . . why'd they do that?"

McTiennan seemed happy to explain. At least he didn't seem to suspect anything. "Just a hunch! When we knocked on it, we noticed it sounded hollow!"

Irma hoped the smile that she had pasted across her face looked relaxed and natural. "Oh, right! And did you . . . did you find anything?"

Irma's dad shrugged. "Nope, nothing! In

fact, I'm just going over to assess the damage."

"Oh, come on," Agent McTiennan teased Mr. Lair. "It's just a little hole in the wall. . . ."

"But I still need to do a report! Should we get going?" Mr. Lair replied.

Irma let out the breath she didn't even realize she'd been holding. Now that she had all the information, she couldn't wait for the agents to leave.

But suddenly Agent Medina had her hand on Irma's shoulder. She ushered Irma away from the car. "Just a moment," she said to her partner and Irma's dad. Medina's eyes looked huge behind her thick glasses, but they remained focused steadily on Irma. "Irma, what do you think we should have found?" Medina demanded.

Irma took a deep breath before she answered. "Nothing, actually! See you around, huh?" she said breezily. She thought she sounded convincing. And she knew Medina wouldn't stop her as she headed into the house—after all, Irma's dad was standing right there. Irma even hummed a little tune, to let Medina know how carefree she was feeling. She wasn't sure if the humming sounded believable, but at least the two agents and her dad were driving away.

"Whew!" Irma breathed as the door shut behind her. She leaned against it, just in case. She'd have to be careful of Medina. That had been a close call.

She closed her eyes and relaxed for a minute. Suddenly she remembered that, when the girls defeated Phobos, the Oracle had made the portals disappear. Cornelia had cast a magic spell to protect the passageway behind the wall in Elyon's basement . . . but when the Oracle closed the portals, surely he had broken Cornelia's spell, too. The agents would probably find only a bunch of rubble there. Nothing to worry about.

But with those two detectives snooping around, who knew what might happen? Irma asked herself, walking down the hall to hang up her coat. Then she sighed. It occurred to her that once she would have told her fellow Guardians everything. Now she wondered when—and if!—she'd even see them again.

Irma could feel the adrenaline wear off after her encounter with the agents. She felt depressed all over again. She remembered how she had once felt, when she was in Meridian with her friends. Meridian had been dark and gloomy before Elyon became the queen. Irma always knew they had important work to do there, but she had always found the place depressing. Now she found Heatherfield depressing, too. No place looked good without her friends.

Driiing! The doorbell rang shrilly, and Irma shouted, "Coming, Dad!"

Why can't he *ever* remember his keys? Irma thought, giggling.

She opened the door absentmindedly, expecting to see her dad standing on the porch with his hand stuck out, waiting for his keys. But when she opened the door, her dad was nowhere to be found. Instead, Will, Hay Lin, and Taranee were standing there.

Will was avoiding Irma's gaze by looking off to the side as if something in the corner of the porch were so interesting that she couldn't tear her gaze away. And Hay Lin was sulking, looking up toward the clouds. Only Taranee looked straight at Irma, with a big, cheery grin and a slight wave of her hand.

The earlier events of the day came flooding

back to Irma, and she quickly turned around, determined to sulk. Though she wanted to tell the girls about her conversation with the Interpol agents, she couldn't get past her hurt feelings. She was angry, and she wasn't about to give in easily. With her back to her friends, she crossed her arms over her chest. And she certainly wasn't going to speak to them without an apology!

THREE

Taranee could tell that Irma was boiling mad. Her friend had power over water, and it wouldn't have surprised Taranee if smoke had begun pouring out of the top of Irma's head!

When Irma got mad, she could get very steamy.

"What's this? Gang-Up-On-Irma Day?" Irma huffed.

Taranee took a deep breath. She had known when she decided to play the peacemaker that it would be a difficult role. But she was sick of the way her friends had been sniping at one another. It had seemed as if the smallest thing set everyone off. Was she the only one who remembered what they'd learned on their last visit to Candracar? Or what they had been like before the Veil had been removed and their friendship had started to fray?

It was as if the Heart of Candracar had sensed a trace of darkness in the girls' friendship, and now their powers weren't working in quite the same manner as they had before. Maybe it was because the girls hadn't always used their powers in the right way. Maybe it was because, recently, they couldn't seem to manage to stick together. Whatever it was, apparently the Oracle was leaving it up to them to fix the problem.

Nobody else seemed to be doing much to help the situation, Taranee thought. But she was determined not to let their powers lapse. Who knew what they might be called upon to do next? Their powers had to be at the ready—so their friendship had to be fixed. Besides, Taranee missed having her friends around. She missed Hay Lin's spontaneous sense of fun, Irma's jokes, Will's sense of adventure, and Cornelia's calm manner.

More urgently, though, the girls had to do everything they could—*everything*—to keep Will from leaving town.

Taranee couldn't put up with Irma's attitude for another second. "Hang on!" she said. "Before we start fighting again, Will's got something to tell you."

Hay Lin nudged Will. Will cleared her throat. "Yeah, well, I'm sorry," she muttered.

Not very convincing, Taranee thought.

Irma wasn't going for it. "How touching!" she exclaimed. "I'm too choked up to reply."

Taranee wished her telepathy were working the way it had used to. It would have come in handy right about then. She would have privately encouraged Will to be nice and apologize so that they could move on.

But suddenly Will changed her tone, with no coaching from her friend. "Taranee made me realize that your idea is the only idea—whatever it is," Will admitted.

Irma looked over at Hay Lin, who was gazing off to the side. She didn't seem to want even to look at Irma.

"Taranee asked me to put up with you all," Hay Lin said. She shook her long hair and put her hand on her hip. "I'm here as a favor to her!"

It wasn't the message of unity that Taranee

had had in mind. But she let it go—it was more important to build the case for hearing Irma's idea. Taranee was willing to bet it involved using their powers. It seemed the only way.

"In this situation," Taranee said, "if we used our powers, we'd be doing it to stay together." Taranee wanted to make that point clear. Irma had been known to use her powers for personal reasons . . . and get herself into trouble in the process.

Irma turned around to face the girls, but she still seemed suspicious. She frowned. "Your reasoning is flawless," she said. "What's the catch?"

Taranee clenched her hands and made a wish. Maybe this was going to work. "When you suggested we go into Simultech, did you have some kind of plan in mind?" she asked, prodding Irma.

"How did you think we'd manage to break into that fortress?" Will said, before Irma had a chance to answer. "By turning ourselves invisible? By flying?"

Taranee wished Will hadn't sounded quite so sarcastic. They all really needed Irma's help. After all, Irma had had a good idea—the only good idea that any of them had come up with so far.

A small smirk spread across Irma's face, and her eyes twinkled. "Actually, I was thinking of something far less magical!" she said.

In a flash, Irma grabbed her coat off the rack in the hallway. Then she sprang out the door, nearly running her friends over. "Follow me! The next bus downtown leaves in two minutes!" she yelled as she sprinted down the street.

Will and Hay Lin didn't budge until Taranee pushed them in the same direction.

The girls reached the stop just as the bus was closing its doors. When Irma smiled, though, nobody could resist—the bus driver looked at the girls and reopened the door without complaint.

"So, Irma," Will said when they were all on the bus, "what's the plan?"

"Let's just pretend we're going to visit your mom at her office," Irma replied. "She'll eat it up. Trust me."

Taranee looked at Will. *Don't back out now,* she warned her friend with her eyes. *There's too much riding on this.*

"Why didn't I think of that?" asked Will.

Irma got the last laugh this time. "Simple! You're not me!" she said.

Taranee would have breathed a sigh of a relief if she hadn't still been panting from their run for the bus. She hoped this plan worked.

Soon the girls were standing outside the glass doors to Simultech's lobby. Simultech occupied all twenty floors of a new office building on the outskirts of town, and security was pretty tight. A voice that came through a silver box asked the girls to state their names and business.

Will shrugged and put on an enthusiastic voice. They were just supposed to be there for fun, after all. "Hi, there! I'm Susan Vandom's daughter," she shouted into the eye of the security camera.

Nothing happened. Taranee guessed that, next, Will's mom would come outside and get them. But instead, suddenly, a woman in a blue suit and cat's-eye glasses tottered toward them on high heels. She sounded even more chipper than Will had sounded—and that was saying a lot. The woman waved wildly at Will.

"Hi, Will!" the woman called.

Will strode over to shake the woman's hand. "Nice to meet you!" she said. "You must be Amanda, my mom's assistant." Will gestured at the other girls and added, "These are my friends."

As the woman, who was, in fact, Amanda, led the girls inside, she grinned over her shoulder. "You little cuties!" she cooed. "Follow me, and don't be intimidated. From out here, Simultech looks like some kind of fortress! But on the inside it's *reeeeally* different."

Irma rolled her eyes at Taranee when Amanda wasn't looking. "Cuties?" she whispered.

Taranee didn't respond—she was too busy looking around the lobby. It was huge, with windows on every side and a ceiling that was several stories high. A few couches were scattered around for people to sit in while waiting for appointments with Simultech personnel, and giant flat-screened TV sets took up most of the space on the huge walls.

Taranee whistled "Woo-hoo!"

"*Way cool!*" said Hay Lin.

"Way cool! Hee-hee! Way cool!" Amanda repeated.

Was Amanda for real? Taranee rolled her eyes at Hay Lin when Amanda wasn't looking.

As they boarded the elevator, Amanda winked at the girls. "I was young once, too, you know!" she said with a giggle.

"Reeeaally?" Irma asked.

Irma was clearly overreacting, and Taranee knew that Will was not happy with the way Irma the drama queen was behaving. Will pinched Irma's arm and gave her a stern look.

"Ouch," Irma whispered.

"Sure!" Amanda droned on. "At your age I always hung out with a whole pack of girl-friends."

Irma patted her arm, sore from Will's pinch. "Did your 'pack' include an animal that bit, too?" she asked as she glared at Will.

Amanda couldn't stop giggling. "Hee-hee! Pack! Animals! I get it! Hee-hee!"

Taranee waited for the explosion between Will and Irma. But it never came. Okay, Taranee realized, at least we're all on the same side where Amanda is concerned. She was in hospitality overdrive!

The glass elevator sped up to the very top of the office building. When the doors opened,

Amanda led the girls down a long hallway. From a safe distance behind her, Irma imitated Amanda's mincing walk.

At last they came to a closed door. Amanda knocked, and Will's mom appeared.

Taranee didn't think she'd have recognized her if she had seen her on the street—Mrs. Vandom looked much more glamorous at work than she did at home. She was wearing a stylish gray suit and big hoop earrings. She even had her hair down. It was long, dark, and wavy, not at all like Will's red mop.

Mrs. Vandom also looked as though she didn't know what to make of the situation. Taranee thought that Will probably didn't come to the office to visit her mother very often.

"Will! Girls!" Mrs. Vandom exclaimed nervously. "What a surprise! What brings you here?"

Will spoke almost in a whisper. "Um, I wanted to talk to you about something important, Mom."

Her mom took the bait. "Okay, Will . . . well . . . come right in." She waved the other girls in, too.

"Thanks, but we'll wait here," Hay Lin said.

Taranee stifled a giggle when Amanda assured Will she'd look after her friends. "I'll keep your friends company! Isn't it just, like, totally cool?"

"Oh, no!" Irma whispered to Taranee. "Now she's starting in on the teen wannabe words again!"

Will gave her friends a quick glance and then followed her mom into the office.

Nobody had counted on Amanda's desk being right outside Mrs. Vandom's office. But otherwise things were pretty much going according to plan. Irma and Hay Lin would search Mrs. Vandom's boss's office while Will kept her mom occupied—and away from their investigation. All they needed was to find the transfer orders and they were home free.

For the millionth time Taranee was re-minded of the reasons the girls had to stick together. Their friendship was too special to lose. Their powers were too precious. They couldn't keep on fighting with one another. And, most important, somehow they would have to reconnect with Cornelia. But first they had to stop Mrs. Vandom from leaving Heatherfield and taking Will away.

Now that Will and her mom had started talking, the other girls would have to move quickly.

Amanda invaded Hay Lin's personal space and got ready for a girl-to-girl chat. She crouched down next to Hay Lin's seat. "So, tell me," she cooed. "Any hunks at school sweet on you?"

"It's like talking to a dinosaur that doesn't know it's extinct!" Irma murmured to Hay Lin.

Taranee settled in to a chair right outside of Mrs. Vandom's office. She strained to hear her and Will talking inside. She imagined that the mood inside the office must have been pretty tense.

"So, Will," Mrs. Vandom was saying now. "What's going on?"

Taranee could make out Will's answer. "Nothing," Will said. "I just wanted to get you to change your mind about the transfer."

Taranee could only imagine what Mrs. Vandom was thinking. She and Will had no doubt talked about this many times already. Taranee's mom would have blown her lid. Even though she was a judge, she was sometimes not very impartial or calm when it came to her own daughter—and especially when it came to her feelings concerning Taranee's crush, Nigel. Judge Cook was not a big fan of his, and she let Taranee know how she felt about him at every opportunity.

Mrs. Vandom seemed to have much more patience than that. Taranee didn't hear any of the screaming she would have expected after Will's opening line.

"We've already talked about it," Mrs. Vandom said sweetly. "In a little while the committee is going to discuss my request."

"I know! That's why I'm here!" Will cried.

Just when things were getting interesting, the two voices grew softer. Taranee hoped that that meant Will was starting a long conversation that would keep her mom tied up for a while.

In the meantime, Amanda had not stopped talking. She didn't seem to notice that Taranee wasn't responding. When she could no longer hear Will's conversation, Taranee turned her attention back to Amanda.

"Oh, how dreamy!" Amanda babbled. "Where did you get those pants? And that adorable sweater?"

Taranee wondered whether she should tell her the name of the store. She was sure Amanda wouldn't think twice about marching into the trendiest shop in the mall. But Taranee couldn't have told her even if she had wanted to—she couldn't get a word in edgewise. Now Amanda was on to hair.

"Listen, I was thinking of getting some purple streaks in my hair!" she confided. "You don't think they clash with clothes too much, do you?"

Taranee bit her tongue to make sure that she didn't burst out laughing. She couldn't laugh when she was biting her tongue, she reasoned.

Just when Taranee thought that she was going to lose it, she saw Hay Lin stand up and approach Amanda. "Ma'am, where's Levin Bishop's office?" she asked.

Amanda was so clueless that she didn't think twice about giving directions. "His office is down there, dear!" she said. "At the end of the hall, on your right."

Hay Lin thanked her and took off as fast as she could, with Irma right behind her.

"I really think she's got a screw loose," Irma

whispered as she walked out the door.

"Better for us!" Hay Lin said. Then she looked over at Taranee. "Now, cover for me, while I go take a look in that office!"

Taranee nodded. But she wished that she were roaming the building looking for Mrs. Vandom's transfer orders instead of listening to a middle-aged woman pretend she was young again. Still, Taranee knew it was all for a good reason. Anything was worth it to help keep Will in Heatherfield and to keep the Guardians together. Looking at Mrs. Vandom's closed office door, she just hoped that Irma's plan worked, and that Will would be able to stay.

FOUR

Inside Mr. Bishop's office, Hay Lin checked every place she could think of—the desk, the file cabinets, even the area under the fancy leather seat-cushions. She tried to keep calm as she ran her hand through her long black hair. She couldn't help feeling panicked. She had to find that letter!

Where is it? she thought. *There are hardly any files or papers anywhere in this office.*

Hay Lin wasn't feeling as confident about the plan as she had been earlier. Rummaging through an office when some high-level security system was possibly spying on her did not make her feel at ease. But she had to do her part.

Hay Lin opened the desk drawers again,

just in case she'd missed something the first time around. There was the same old box of paper clips and assorted pens, and there were a few pads of paper.

It seemed impossible to Hay Lin that she and her friends had once closed portals and battled strange creatures, to save Meridian with their super powers.

Too bad that my power over air can't help me locate Mrs. Vandom's letter! Hay Lin thought. *At least in the previous Guardian battles, I knew how to use my magic to complete a mission.*

Suddenly it occurred to Hay Lin that keeping Will in Heatherfield—and someday, somehow, getting through to Cornelia—might be their newest mission. The realization made Hay Lin think that this might be one of their most important tasks yet.

As she looked over the spotless desk, she sighed. She wished the fashionable goggles on her head could see through furniture and files to help her locate the letter. If she could have found it, then Mr. Bishop wouldn't have been able to accept Mrs. Vandom's resignation. She had to keep looking!

"Nothing!" Hay Lin mumbled to herself as she stood helplessly in the center of the room. "I checked everywhere. But no letters! No files! Nothing!" She clenched her fist in disgust.

Suddenly, the door to the office opened with a creak, and Irma stuck her head in. "The safe!" she whispered. Irma popped inside the office and pointed to a painting on the wall. "Mr. Bishop keeps his documents in a safe behind that painting."

Hay Lin gaped for a minute. How could Irma possibly know that? Then she realized . . .

"Wait," she whispered. "Don't tell me! You just went and asked Amanda!"

Irma grinned.

Hay Lin wasn't sure if Irma had actually asked Amanda or if all those hours Irma had spent watching her favorite TV show, *Spygirl*, had given her the idea.

As she helped Hay Lin take the painting down, Irma looked very proud. "Amanda's brain must not be connected to her mouth!" she said.

I guess she did just ask the babble-head! Hay Lin mused.

She wondered if Amanda had any clue as to

what she had just told Irma.

Once they had lifted the painting off the wall, Hay Lin was able to reach a silver door with a little dial in the center. Hay Lin had to give Irma credit. She'd never have thought to look there without Amanda's tip.

"So, do you know the combination to this thing, too?" Hay Lin asked.

Irma came up short this time. "Nope," she replied. "And I don't know a good safecracker, either."

Just then Hay Lin heard a sound at the door. She flattened herself against the wall under the painting. Was it the security guards she'd been dreading? Was it Will's mom, demanding to know why they were rummaging around in her boss's office? Hay Lin scanned the room quickly, but there was no place to hide. . . .

The door opened, and Will rushed in, with Taranee close behind her. Will took one look at the exposed safe and seemed to assess the whole situation very quickly. "Let's use our magic!" she cried. "Isn't that what we'd decided we'd do?"

"Will! Taranee!" Irma exclaimed. "This office is getting crowded."

Taranee stifled a giggle when Amanda assured Will she'd look after her friends. "I'll keep your friends company! Isn't it just, like, totally cool?"

"Oh, no!" Irma whispered to Taranee. "Now she's starting in on the teen wannabe words again!"

Will gave her friends a quick glance and then followed her mom into the office.

Nobody had counted on Amanda's desk being right outside Mrs. Vandom's office. But otherwise things were pretty much going according to plan. Irma and Hay Lin would search Mrs. Vandom's boss's office while Will kept her mom occupied—and away from their investigation. All they needed was to find the transfer orders and they were home free.

For the millionth time Taranee was re-minded of the reasons the girls had to stick together. Their friendship was too special to lose. Their powers were too precious. They couldn't keep on fighting with one another. And, most important, somehow they would have to reconnect with Cornelia. But first they had to stop Mrs. Vandom from leaving Heatherfield and taking Will away.

Amanda led the girls down a long hallway. From a safe distance behind her, Irma imitated Amanda's mincing walk.

At last they came to a closed door. Amanda knocked, and Will's mom appeared.

Taranee didn't think she'd have recognized her if she had seen her on the street—Mrs. Vandom looked much more glamorous at work than she did at home. She was wearing a styl-ish gray suit and big hoop earrings. She even had her hair down. It was long, dark, and wavy, not at all like Will's red mop.

Mrs. Vandom also looked as though she didn't know what to make of the situation. Taranee thought that Will probably didn't come to the office to visit her mother very often.

"Will! Girls!" Mrs. Vandom exclaimed ner-vously. "What a surprise! What brings you here?"

Will spoke almost in a whisper. "Um, I wanted to talk to you about something impor-tant, Mom."

Her mom took the bait. "Okay, Will . . . well . . . come right in." She waved the other girls in, too.

"Thanks, but we'll wait here," Hay Lin said.

Hay Lin was glad to have some backup. It almost felt like old times, with her friends at her side, all of them working together. Except for one minor thing, Hay Lin thought sadly: we're the Power of Five—not four. Hay Lin missed her friend Cornelia and wished that she were there to help as well.

"It's about to get worse!" Will said urgently. "Mr. Bishop is in my mom's office! They've decided to start the meeting early."

Taranee opened the door about a millimeter to see what was going on outside the office. "He's in the hallway!" she reported. "He'll be here to pick up his papers very soon." She quietly shut the door again and turned to Hay Lin.

Hay Lin looked at her friends and knew suddenly what she had to do. She lifted her arms in the air and closed her eyes. In the most confident voice she could muster, Hay Lin announced her plan. "I'll take care of this. Leave it to me."

I need to focus and call upon the powers of air, she thought.

Taking a deep breath, she found herself in the center of a familiar, gentle wind.

"First of all," she said, with more confidence

than she felt, "I'll soundproof the room."

As Hay Lin's magic swirled into action, the few papers piled on Mr. Bishop's desk began to fly around the office. The turbulent air created a stormy cloud that made it seem as if a tornado were unfolding.

It's working! Hay Lin thought triumphantly.

It felt amazing to have that surge of power once again—it had been a while since Hay Lin had felt that incredible feeling sweep through her body. Now, with a tremendous gust of air, she tried to break open Mr. Bishop's safe.

Throwing her hands in front of her body with a mighty force, she felt as though she were pushing the air to knock down the door. The air obeyed her command and rushed toward the safe.

Swoosh!

The mighty gust became a gentle breeze, and the papers sank to the floor. Hay Lin opened her eyes.

The safe was still locked.

Irma stroked her head, trying to tame her windblown locks. "Congratulations!" she said. "If you were trying to mess up our hair, you did a great job."

A minute earlier, Hay Lin would have laughed at Irma's quip about her hair. But now she was too stunned to care. She looked down at her hands. The power of air had never failed her before. Usually she was able with great ease to summon the power to control her element. What was happening?

Gazing down at her hands again, she felt as if she were waiting for the others to tell her what had happened. Then she looked up at her friends, searching their faces for an answer. "But . . . I don't get it. . . . I concentrated on the safe, and . . ."

"And nothing happened!" Taranee said, finishing her thought. "Our powers are coming and going."

"Go ahead and say it!" Irma challenged Taranee. "They're at an all-time low!"

From their glum faces, Hay Lin guessed that her friends were feeling as low as she was just then. Will surprised her by narrowing her eyes and raising her fists in the air. Will had the most to lose of any of them. Maybe that was why she was so sure of herself.

"Let's transform!" Will said. "Joining our powers is the only way we can manage to do anything without Cornelia here."

The Heart of Candracar appeared in the palm of Will's hand. The crystal orb was radiating a vibrant pink burst of energy. For what seemed like a long moment, Hay Lin worried that the Heart of Candracar wouldn't work this time, either. But then, just as she always had, Will reached into the air—and there was the Heart.

"Heart of Candracar," Will shouted fiercely. "Help us!"

"Fire!" Taranee shouted.

"Water!" Irma yelled.

"Air!" Hay Lin cried.

As Will's hand closed around the Heart, Mr. Bishop's office was filled with a brilliant, intense light. Great sparks emanated from the crystal as the four powers united into one awesome force.

Hay Lin wondered what would happen without Cornelia present. The girls weren't used to being one short. Would things work as they always had?

Hay Lin had her answer when the light faded and all that remained was a pinkish afterglow. Hay Lin looked down, and there they were: her luminescent wings, her silky purple shirt, and her blue top that bared her belly in just the right place. Her trademark goggles were no longer lodged on the top of her head—instead, her black hair lay smooth and straight. Hay Lin was always blown away by the transformation that happened when her friends used their powers. Feeling like a new person inside as well as out, she was ready to conquer the world.

"See?" Will said, looking down at her taller, stronger body.

Hay Lin smiled at her friend. She knew that Will must be feeling incredibly relieved. All of them were.

"We haven't lost our powers completely," Will added.

"Looks like we haven't," Taranee agreed. She crossed her arms and looked at her wings as if she thought they might disappear at any minute. "But what do we do now?"

Hay Lin glanced at Irma, hoping she'd have an idea, but Irma was still marveling over her own transformation. Hay Lin popped her head out of the office for a split second, careful not to be spotted. When she looked down the hallway, she gasped. "Whatever it is, it's got to be quick! Mr. Bishop's here!"

Mr. Bishop was a middle-aged man with a shiny bald head and glasses that slid halfway down his nose. He didn't look much like any foe they'd fought recently, Hay Lin thought, but he could prove to be more formidable than any of them. He alone had the power to separate Will from the rest of the Guardians.

He didn't sound particularly scary, though. Right outside his office he could be heard talking to Will's mother.

"So it's decided then, Susan," he said.

"Thank you so much, Levin," Mrs. Vandom said. The girls heard her heels clicking on the shiny floor as she headed back to her office. Hay Lin turned her attention back to her friends. She knew that they had to act quickly.

"Let's concentrate on the safe!" Will said. "When I count three . . ."

Will didn't finish her sentence. The girls heard the doorknob turning. Mr. Bishop was on the other side—coming in!

There was no time to plan what they would do once they broke in to the safe. There was no time to discuss transforming themselves back again before Mr. Bishop saw them. Now, as on so many occasions in the past, they were just going to have to trust in their powers.

As Will counted, Hay Lin conjured up a white swirl of pure magic and stood beside her friends, facing the safe. Irma's blue magic shone on one side of her, with Will's pink magic and Taranee's orange magic glowing on the other side. Suddenly Hay Lin felt more confident than she had since she'd walked into Simultech. She and her friends were going to accomplish this task *together*. They would blast that safe open. They would grab—or destroy—the papers. Either way, they'd make sure Will and her mom stayed put in Heatherfield.

On the count of three, the four girls directed the full force of their collective power toward the wall. The power homed in on the safe and blasted it into a million pieces. Hay Lin was braced for the aftershock, but even so, she careened into the opposite wall of the office.

Plaster rained down on the floor, and scraps of paper flew through the air like confetti. Two of the other girls—she couldn't tell which—hovered near the ceiling before they finally crash-landed on the rug.

Hay Lin covered her eyes to protect them from the blast. She waited for the debris to clear so that she could see what was left where the safe had been. Feeling more disoriented than she usually did after using her magic, Hay Lin struggled to get a sense of what was happening. She was very confused. Was it because the floor was still reverberating from the shock of the explosion? Was it because her ears were ringing? There was a high-pitched noise swirling around her head.

Weee! Weee! Weee!

Looking around, Hay Lin realized that she was hearing a fire alarm. A very loud fire alarm.

Something had gone wrong. Really wrong.

FIVE

Will felt her body slam down on to the ground with a mighty force. She lay still for a minute as she tried to catch her breath.

What happened? she thought, rubbing her head.

She had been holding the Heart in her hand, and everything had felt right. The power had seemed to be working, and the welcome transformation had occurred. And then, there had been an explosion.

Will raised her head and saw Irma, Taranee, and Hay Lin lying on the ground near her. They seemed to be all right, but they were no longer in their Guardian forms. The magical green and purple outfits had disappeared, replaced by their usual clothes.

What is going on? Will wondered. And what is that awful wailing sound?

Weee! Weee! Weee!

Oh, no, Will thought. The fire alarm!

Will clearly pictured the scene happening outside the office.

Her mom would be demanding to know why the floor was shaking and the fire alarm blaring. She would shake Amanda and then Mr. Bishop until they told her where her daughter and her daughter's friends had gone. Will's mom was obsessed with personal safety—she ran fire drills at home, the way teachers and firefighters always said people should. If her she had thought Will was in danger, she would have stopped at nothing to find her and make sure that she was safe.

As the dust finally settled, Will reached up, placed a hand on her sore head, and looked around at the damage. "What a blow!" she exclaimed. "Is everybody still in one piece?"

It was hard to hear what Hay Lin was saying above the din of the fire alarm. Will strained to hear her friend's words.

"I'm okay!" Hay Lin shouted, finally yelling loud enough for Will to hear her. "I just hope the soundproofing worked."

Will hoped so, too. If not, everyone on that floor of Simultech—or, she thought, let's face it, everyone in the whole building—would be wondering what had happened inside Mr. Bishop's office.

This was a setback that Will had not expected. Why was nothing going right? Then Will had a funny thought, and she couldn't help grinning. If someone had walked into the office at that moment, how would they have even begun to explain what they were doing in the middle of the chaos?

"Think how funny it would be if someone came in and saw this mess!" Will said, trying to lighten the mood.

Hay Lin and Irma smiled awkwardly. But Taranee ignored Will's question. She looked panicked as she examined her changed body. "Why have we gone back to our normal selves?" she asked.

Will's heart sank as she tried to come up with an answer. Obviously the girls had worked some magic just then. But if they couldn't even stay transformed, they had a serious problem on their hands.

Suddenly, there was silence, which gave Irma the perfect excuse to change the subject. "Oh, the alarm's finally stopped! Good going, Hay Lin."

"Too bad it wasn't me who shut it off!" Hay Lin snapped. "I tried, but it didn't work."

Will felt a drop of water run down her back. Was that sweat? She wondered.

No . . . it was the sprinklers on the ceiling, part of the fire safety system for the building. Just what they needed. Will felt the entire situation slipping from her control—as if she had ever really been in control in the first place.

"Why don't you do something?" Hay Lin said to Irma. "After all, water's your element."

It was obvious to Will that Hay Lin's patience was wearing thin. All three girls looked to Irma to see if she could stop the emergency sprinkler.

"Okay, okay," Irma said with a slight shrug. A little water had never bothered her. "All this fuss over a little drizzle!" She raised her arms to stop the water. But instead of stopping, the sprinkler went on spurting water. Irma looked shocked and very confused.

"Hey!" Irma cried out. "What's happening?

Or, better yet, what's not happening?"

"Forget that stuff about our powers coming and going!" Taranee said as she went to stand next to Irma. "They're completely gone!"

Will felt a shiver down her back. The girls' powers had never truly failed them before. And now it seemed to be happening all the time. She gazed at the hole in the wall where the safe had been.

All this mess started because of me, Will thought. What kind of trouble have I gotten everyone into? And to make matters worse, we're losing our powers. How did this happen?

Before Will could verbalize all of her worries to her friends she noticed something different about Mr. Bishop's office. The large hole where the safe had been had smoke streaming out of it. Squinting to see through the billowing smoke, Will noticed a bright yellow light, which was creating an eerie glow. There was a big, blue blob taking the form of a person, and it was staring right at her!

Will blinked. The thing was still there when she opened her eyes, so it wasn't a figment of her imagination. She shivered, but it wasn't because she was soaked by the sprinklers.

"G—guys! Look over there!" she called out to her friends. "Look where the safe was!"

Irma's back was to the hole in the wall, and she was so preoccupied with her water-power shortage that she didn't seem to give Will's exclamation a thought. She put her hands on her hips and rolled her eyes. "I just don't get it!" she exclaimed. "This water is simply not obeying me!"

Exasperated, Will pointed her finger, urging Irma to turn around. The blue creature was getting bigger and bigger.

"What's the big deal, Will?" Irma asked without turning around. "The safe blew up! So what?"

Will's eyes grew wider. She watched in horror as the blue thing started taking shape.

"Irma!" Will blurted out, trying desperately to get her friend to turn around.

"We didn't mean to do that much damage," Irma said with a shrug. She was still not paying attention to Will's frantic pointing and horrified expression. "It's just how things turned out."

"Irma!" Will yelled. "You'd better turn around and take a look!"

"Oh, come on!" Irma said with a dismissive

wave of her hand. "The letter was destroyed, and now all you have to do is tell your . . ." Irma turned her back as she gestured to the wall where the safe had once been lodged. As Irma turned, Will saw that she was finally witnessing the bizarre scene behind her.

"MAAAAAAMA!" Irma screamed when she saw what was behind her.

The creature had quickly transformed into a perfect replica of Irma!

Irma was so scared she practically knocked Will over. "What is it? What is it?" she yelled.

"How should I know?" Will shot back. "Irma, stop screaming!"

Hay Lin confirmed what they had all seen. "That thing looked just like Irma!" she pointed out, deliberately backing away from the creepy creature. It shifted as she spoke.

The blob reminded Will of something she'd given her mom for her birthday once—a little pink ball you were supposed to squeeze in order to relieve tension. You could even draw a face in it if you poked it with a pencil, but eventually the thing would revert to its original shape.

Now the current blob had taken on some

new features. Taranee was the first to realize what was going on. "That's you, Hay Lin!" she exclaimed.

The thing's face looked just like Hay Lin's; it advanced ever closer to the girls, still changing, more quickly this time. Now it was glaring at Taranee.

"Uh-oh!" she screamed. The blob had taken on the form of Taranee, right down to her glasses and assorted braids with colored beads. "I think it's angry with me now!"

Will watched the thing as it moved away from Taranee and came slowly to face her. It morphed again. This was freakier than any late-night TV show or science-fiction book, Will thought, watching as the blob reflected her image: it had her red hair and brown eyes.

"It's like being reflected in a 3-D mirror!" Will said. Many questions raced through her mind. What was happening? "I don't get it!" she cried.

Her curiosity turned into rage, and she felt herself gathering courage to speak. Though she was petrified of the morphing blue blob, she clenched her fists and tried to speak with confidence. "Who are you?" she demanded, addressing the creature. "What do you want?"

The blob didn't answer. Instead, it leaped to the other side of Mr. Bishop's office, moving toward the windows! The creature no longer had a face, but it certainly had a plan to carry out. Will didn't even want to consider all the mischief the creature might manage to cause if it were free to roam the streets.

"No! Stop!" Will shrieked.

The creature pressed its faceless blue head against one of the windows and appeared to look down at the parking lot below. And then . . . it jumped!

Will raced to the window and looked down. Mr. Bishop's office was on the top floor. Normally, the view would have provided a nice break from a busy workday. But right now it resembled a scene out of an action-adventure movie. Only here there was no stunt double acting out the part.

Searching the ground, Will strained to see where the morphing blue blob had gone. "It . . . it just did something that's impossible," Will stammered as she continued to survey the parking lot. Then she spotted the creature. It looked like a giant, blue, clay sculpture that was not quite finished. There was no face, and there were no defining characteristics, but the thing certainly could move. And it was racing straight toward downtown Heatherfield! "It's running at an inhuman pace!"

Will hung her head in despair. She was speechless. Her head was spinning.

As if this day weren't already a complete disaster, she thought, now we've let a monster escape into the city.

"That's like nothing we've ever seen!" Taranee pointed out. "Not even in Meridian."

"Do you . . . do you think we let it in when we blasted open the safe?" Hay Lin asked.

"I'm worried that we *made* it," Will said slowly. "Our magic has been out of whack recently. What if we *created* this thing, by mistake?"

"The bigger question is, what's it made of?" asked Taranee. "It can take on any shape, I guess. But you can stick your hands right through it."

Hay Lin nodded. "Maybe it's just a blob of energy."

"But a blob of energy that can look just like any one of us," Will added. "And probably do things that we might not want to do."

Irma, who had been very quiet, looked around at her friends. "Well," she said. "I've got a funny feeling we just caused some trouble."

Will agreed. She just wondered how much trouble.

SIX

Luba gazed into a pool that allowed her to use her powers to see and hear everything that happened in Heatherfield. With great interest she watched the scene displayed in the still waters of the pool. She'd been observing the five Guardians carefully for a while now. She'd been watching and scheming, hoping that things would unfold as she had planned. Luba rubbed her hands together in delight as she watched the latest events involving the young Guardians. Things were working out much better then she could ever have hoped.

"Yes, girls," Luba drawled. "Without meaning to, that's exactly what you've done—you've created big trouble. You've given life to an Altermere!"

Luba whirled around to take another look at the sphere hovering in the Aura Hall, where the Aurameres had once been. Where once five droplets of magical essence had been suspended in a magical orb, a lumpy mass now hung in one place, spinning. Four Aurameres were fused together, as Luba observed with a morbid sort of satisfaction. And the green one had broken free. This was the natural outgrowth of the girls' weakness, she told herself. She'd simply helped it along a little. . . .

Luba thought back to the moment when she had conceived her brilliant idea. The Aurameres had dwindled until they were practically nothing, and, no matter what she did, the Oracle no longer heeded Luba's warnings about the seriousness of the situation. So Luba had grown angrier and angrier. Then she'd noticed that four of the five Aurameres were hurtling ever closer to one another. The Aurameres always did this when the girls were about to unite their powers with the same purpose or intention. But the Aurameres were never supposed to collide. Luba knew full well that there was great danger in allowing the Aurameres to collide. But letting the collision occur was all part of her plan.

"The only Auramere to keep its distance is Cornelia's," she whispered to herself. "Her friends must not have involved her in this mission. But it makes no difference. Four Aurameres will suffice! Now that they are so close, all I need to do is bring them together with magic . . . and wait for the four Guardians to use their powers."

Already her plan had gone much more smoothly than she could ever have hoped. As she watched the Guardians try to open the office safe, she had waited patiently for their powers to be united. The powerful surge had been even greater than anything Luba had hoped for.

Ah, Luba thought happily as she had witnessed the scene: the Guardians' powers, joined together strongly.

As the Aurameres had drawn dangerously close together in the magical sphere, Luba had been able to watch the rise of the Altermere. Her intervention had proved successful. With the Aurameres just inches apart, the four separate powers had combined. At that point, Luba's magic had sprung from her fingers, looping around each Auramere and binding it to the next in an intricate knot.

The Aurameres had behaved just as Luba had expected. When the girls combined their powers to break open Mr. Bishop's safe, the Aurameres had come together, too, forming a single sphere. The explosion that had occurred in the Aura Hall made the explosion in Mr. Bishop's office look like nothing more than a little puff of smoke. Luba had shielded her eyes from the bright volcanic blasts among the Aurameres. And then it was done. The Aurameres had melded together, right there in the Aura Hall.

In Heatherfield, however, the melded powers were destined to take on a new life of their own.

Luba was highly amused to see the girls' reaction to the Altermere. Calling it a blob? Thinking they could follow it? Soon they would learn just how large a problem they had on their hands. Oh, yes, soon they would learn.

Luba needed to inform the Oracle and the Council of the explosion right away. She hurried to the meeting inside the Temple, preparing her announcement and reminding herself not to betray her role in the ruination of the Aurameres. Of course, the Council would see that it was the flaws in the Guardians' abilities that had caused their magic to self-destruct, she reasoned. Nobody would suspect that Luba had had anything to do with it. At last, she gloated, the Council would be forced to see its mistake and to set about finding new Guardians.

The members of the Council were seated in the arena that encircled the Oracle's platform. The Oracle appeared to be meditating, but Luba knew that some part of his mind was focused on the proceedings going on around him. Luba looked up at the tall white pillars that lined the Temple, drawing inspiration from their structure and light. She strongly believed that her decision to interfere with the Guardians' magic was a towering achievement, and that she would soon be rewarded for her work. The Council might not agree with her at first, but it would come to see the wisdom of her ways. The Council needed Guardians it could rely on—not young girls who constantly caused trouble.

When she had collected her thoughts, Luba

asked the Oracle for permission to speak to the group. The Oracle nodded. Luba marched to the center of the gathering and began to speak in a hushed tone.

"Brothers and sisters of the Congregation," she said. "I, Luba, Keeper of the Aurameres, have grave news. The Guardians have lost their powers!"

Immediately the Council began to buzz. The members were aghast at Luba's announcement.

"What? How could this have happened?" one elder of the council asked.

It was Luba's responsibility to guard against this very thing. She threw up her hands as she looked around at the gathered elders. "They freed themselves of their energies, giving life to an Altermere!"

It was mostly true, she knew. She had left out only one part of the story: without her magic, none of it would have happened; the Aurameres would not have disappeared on their own, nor would the Altermere have been created without her interference.

The Council was dumbstruck. A collective murmur arose among the members. They had never heard of anything like this.

"It was all the fault of the young girls," Luba continued. "They were imperfect, and so . . ."

Suddenly a voice roared, "No!"

Luba's eyes widened. She grimaced as she realized that the loud roar had come from the Oracle. He'd been hovering in the center of the Temple, but now he was on his feet, facing her.

"No lies, Luba!" he cried. "I cannot bear them!"

Luba, however, would confess to nothing. She believed that what she was doing was justified and correct. "Oracle! What is upsetting you so?" she asked. She tried to remain calm as she stood before the Congregation.

The Oracle stared sadly at the floor. "I am suffering, my dear friend," he answered. "And you know the reason why!"

The Oracle's deep blue eyes were fixed on Luba; he held her in his gaze. The Oracle's power was quiet, but almost absolute.

Inwardly, Luba squirmed. But she waited to hear what the Oracle would say. Perhaps he didn't know the extent of her involvement.

The Oracle continued, in a voice that was

close to a whisper. "I told you that a test was being given, Luba! But it was *you* who were being put through it, not the Guardians."

Suddenly Luba felt weak. The room started to spin, and she took a step backward, to steady herself.

The Oracle raised his voice. Luba wasn't sure she'd ever heard him do that before.

"It was *you* who brought the Aurameres close together!" he declared.

The Council began to buzz again.

"What?" asked an Elder.

"But that's unheard of!" another Council member cried.

Don't you wish *you'd* dared to have an original idea? Luba asked silently as she looked around at the members of the Council.

Suddenly, she felt defensive.

The Oracle stared at Luba, his eyes boring into hers, and Luba remembered that she was supposed to respond. "I . . . I . . ." she stuttered. Her skin turned red, and her whiskers trembled. This wasn't how triumph should feel, she realized. Had she made a mistake?

The Oracle turned to face the Council while still addressing Luba. His usually calm voice now held a current of anger. "Yes! You did so to make us believe that the Guardians were unsuitable! But in doing so you committed a very grave and irreparable act!"

Luba didn't know much about Altermeres. But the Oracle seemed to think she'd done something dire. Maybe her magic could be undone. That was all that Luba could hope for just then. "Wait!" she exclaimed. "You could . . ."

Her thought was erased by the Oracle's shattering cry.

"I cannot do anything now, Luba!" he screamed, in the loudest voice she'd ever heard come from the usually serene and peaceful being. "You have interfered with fate!"

The Oracle was so angry that his hands were quivering. He took a deep breath and continued. "The Altermere is made of pure power! The power of four of the five Guardians!"

The Council members looked at each other, confused. "This means that the Chosen Ones are now vulnerable!" one of the Elders stated.

Well, of course, Luba thought. That was the idea.

The Oracle shook his head in sorrow. "Yes,"

he agreed. "This is a moment long awaited by dark forces."

Suddenly Luba was overwhelmed by the enormity of what she had done. She had utterly disgraced herself. In saving the world from the Guardians, she might have made the situation much worse, by creating even more danger. Now there was no going back. What price would she have to pay?

Luba reached for the Oracle's robe and tried to apologize. "Oracle, I had no way of knowing that. . . ." she began.

The Oracle raised his hand to stop her speech. "Now, a legendary harmful being walks the earth. The Altermere will seek out the last Guardian. It will find her! And when that time comes, the five powers will be reunited!" His voice wavered with emotion as he finished his furious speech. "And when that happens, not even I will be able to foresee what is to come!"

Luba trembled in fear as she looked over at the Oracle. What trouble had she caused the Guardians? What trouble had she caused the universe?

SEVEN

Cornelia was alone in her bedroom, her elbows propped on her desk, her chin resting in the palms of her hands. Her gaze darted to the window, and for a moment she thought briefly of the world that lay beyond her room. None of it mattered to her now. Then she took a deep breath. All that really mattered was right there in front of her.

Staring at the white flower in the blue glass dish on her desk, Cornelia couldn't help feeling sad. The flower was a painful reminder of her life as a Guardian of the Veil: the battles against Phobos, the rescue of Meridian.

The power of the earth, Cornelia thought, that's what I had. Or what I have, I guess. But it's completely useless if it won't even help bring you back to life, Caleb.

Cornelia couldn't have cared less about her magic. All she wanted was that boy back: the love of her life.

Caleb had been the boy of her dreams, no doubt about it. Cornelia had met him in Meridian, when he was part of the rebel forces fighting against Prince Phobos's evil army. When it came time to restore Elyon to the throne, Caleb was right there by the young princess's side. But his good deed turned out to be his downfall. Caleb had completed his task and helped to make Elyon queen. . . . Then, Phobos had captured him. Phobos ended by sparing Caleb's life, but barely. One of his final acts was to transform Caleb with a sinister spell . . . into this flower.

Cornelia tended faithfully to Caleb in his flower form. She hated to leave him. She believed that without her loving care, Caleb's very soul would die. And Cornelia still hoped that there was some way he would come back to her again . . . as a boy. It was the only thing that kept her going.

A cool breeze blew the long pink curtains in

her window, and Cornelia shivered. She no longer wanted to do any of the things that had once made her happy. Her ice skates hung on the wall, and her phone sat quiet on the desk. She didn't want to do anything—especially talk to anyone. None of her friends truly understood. She didn't feel that anyone really understood what she was going through. Cornelia sighed again. She had never felt so alone in her life.

Once, not long ago, she had had Elyon, her best friend, who had always been there to understand. But now, Elyon was living in another world. Cornelia's other friends had drifted away, too.

Well, maybe Cornelia thought, she had pushed them away. It was too painful to be with them just then. She feared that they would make fun of the way she tended to the flower; of the way she continued to talk to him even though he was a flower; of the way she took care of the delicate, white petals. They would probably just dismiss her lost love as a passing thing, Cornelia thought. But what did they know? Their crushes were on boys right there in Heatherfield. Regular, normal, available boys.

It all seemed just so unfair.

Cornelia picked up her flower and inhaled deeply.

Sometimes I look at you, and I wonder if you ever really existed, she thought sadly.

But just then a very clear vision of Caleb came into her head, and she relaxed a little. She clearly remembered Caleb's embrace and his kiss.

Tump. Tump.

A knock at the door jolted Cornelia out of her reverie. The door swung open. Cornelia's vision of Caleb disappeared in a flash, and she looked up to see her dad standing in the hallway.

"Can I come in?" he asked tentatively.

"Dad, you're home from work early," Cornelia managed to say. She put Caleb on her desk, where he'd be safe—and where he might escape her father's notice.

Mr. Hale was in a great mood. "Yes, I left work early!" he announced. "Being the big, big boss at a bank . . ."

Cornelia had heard it a million times, and so she finished the sentence for her dad: "'. . . also has its advantages!' You always say that, but it's not true, you know."

Her dad ruffled her hair and gave his eldest daughter a big smile. At that moment, Cornelia wished that she could tell her dad everything that had happened to her and about how her heart was bursting with grief. She wished that Caleb could have been there to talk to her father. They would probably have gotten along, Cornelia thought. The two men both had strong convictions, passion, and a great sense of humor. Cornelia looked up at her dad and smiled. It was the first time she could remember smiling in a long time.

"What's that?" asked Cornelia, pointing to a jar in her dad's hands. "Honey?"

Mr. Hale grinned and held up the small jar filled with golden liquid. "Yep," he said, "I spread it all through the house, including the dining room! A little trick to lure a certain bear I know out of its den and to dinner!"

For her dad's sake, Cornelia hoped he was kidding about spreading honey on her mother's carpets. Her mother would have screamed at him. But her dad was a big-time jokester—it was impossible to resist his charm. And it would be impossible to miss dinner again tonight, Cornelia realized. She could only push her family away for so long. She gave her dad a big hug, and followed him through the apartment to the dining room.

Her mom and Lilian were already seated at the table. Quietly, Cornelia took her seat, next to her mother. Usually dinner at the Hale house was boisterous and fun. Lilian would shout or sing, and Cornelia would tell some story about school. But tonight, the sounds of utensils hitting the plates were the only sounds that filled the room.

Tling! Pling! Pling!

Cornelia pushed her cabbage around her plate with her fork.

Finally, her dad broke the silence. "We could use Morse code to communicate with each other!" he joked as he tapped his fork and knife on his plate.

Tling, tling, pling.

"Yes, since all we seem to hear is the noise of the silverware," Cornelia's mom agreed.

Cornelia felt a pang of guilt. After all, her parents were trying to help, by making Cornelia get out of her room—and out of her depressed funk. Maybe she should make an effort and apologize for her silence.

"Sorry," she said quietly. She looked up at her mother and tried to change the subject. "I was just wondering why we're eating dinner so early."

Her dad threw up his hands. Apparently, Cornelia was supposed to have known. "The movies!" he cried. "Your mother and I are taking Lilian to an early show!"

Cornelia's little sister, Lilian, couldn't help chiming in. "Eating early is fine with me!" she exclaimed. "But do I have to eat this cabbage? Bleah!"

For a moment, Cornelia was comforted by the fact that soon everyone would be out of the house and she'd be alone again. Then she could return to her room and feel free to continue talking to Caleb without any interruptions. Now that she knew that her parents were taking Lilian out, she wondered why her dad had made such a big deal about making her come to the dining-room table. Unaware of the time, she had followed him. But when she looked at her watch she realized it was actually very early for dinner. Normally, before they went to an early movie, they would grab sandwiches and eat in the kitchen.

"What I don't get," Cornelia snapped, "is why we *all* have to eat here in the dining room!"

"She's right!" Lilian agreed. "We could have had a sandwich before going like we always do!"

Cornelia's mom studied both of her daughters seriously. "Certain things are done together, as a family," she explained. She pursed her lips in frustration.

Oh, please, Cornelia thought. Spare me.

She was in no mood to pretend that everything was fine. She turned to face her mother.

"Is that why you brought work home with you?" she shot back. Her mom had come home early as well, but with a large, bulging briefcase.

"My renovations lab is closed for . . . um . . ." her mother stuttered, "renovations."

"That's a laugh," Cornelia said. "Go ahead and say it! You just want to keep an eye on me! You feel guilty!"

Mrs. Hale looked genuinely shocked. "Excuse me?" she said. Maybe Cornelia had struck the wrong tone. She didn't want to start a fight. But she was tired of everyone's tiptoeing around her as if she were some kind of invalid.

"Yes, guilty," Cornelia said as she considered the facts. "You've seen me without my friends! Poor little thing, all alone! And you're thinking, What's wrong with her? A big fight with her friends? Problems at school?"

Now that she'd started, Cornelia couldn't stop. Her anger was seething inside of her, and her voice was getting louder and louder. "You're wondering, Did I raise her wrong? Didn't I buy her enough shoes? Clothes? Useless things?"

"That's enough!" Mrs. Hale yelled. "If you didn't keep pushing me away, I could give you a lot more!"

"Like what?" Cornelia demanded. "A nice, fat bank account?"

Mr. Hale speared a forkful of cabbage. With a very serious face he looked at Cornelia. "I can take care of that! After all, I do manage a bank."

Cornelia stared at him. She watched her father's face break into a broad smile, and she couldn't stay angry any longer. In spite of herself, she started laughing. These days, her emotions were totally unpredictable. She felt as though she were riding an emotional roller coaster. But just then, it felt really good to laugh.

Cornelia's mom was laughing, too. "That's just like you, Harold!" she cried, giving her husband a playful slap on the shoulder.

Even Lilian was laughing at her dad. Cornelia turned to her little sister. "What are you laughing about?" she teased. "Since when do you get jokes?"

Lilian gasped for breath. She was giggling in the way that only little kids could. "It's just that Daddy's making a funny face! He looks like Napoleon!"

Cornelia had to admit that at that moment her dad did look a little like the black cat. "You're right!" she said, "now that I think about it." She paused for a second. "Speaking of which, where's . . ."

As if in answer to her question, Cornelia heard a crash upstairs; she suspected the cat right away.

The sound is coming from my room, she thought in panic. And I left my door open!

Her heart racing, Cornelia jumped up from the table. She ran out of the dining room and up the stairs to see what was going on.

Once she reached the top of the stairs, Cornelia realized that she was too late. Napoleon was inside her room. The mischievous cat had knocked over the vase that held Caleb in his flower form, and it had fallen off the desk. The precious flower was in a heap on the floor, surrounded by bits of broken pottery. To make matters worse, Napoleon's face was dangerously close to the fragile petals! Cornelia lunged for the flower

"No!" Cornelia wailed, as she tried to shoo the cat away.

That was why she'd never wanted that bratty cat in the first place, she thought. Even though he was a gift from Will, she knew the cat was trouble. Kneeling on the floor, she reached gently for the flower. It appeared to be in one piece. But had the shock of Napoleon's attack been too much for Caleb? Had the shards of pottery strewn around him cut him? What if Caleb had been seriously hurt? Cornelia was overcome with despair.

She hovered over the flower. "Scat, Napoleon," she hissed, swatting him away more forcefully this time. She was not going to let him get away with that! "Get out, you beast!"

Turning, Cornelia realized that her family stood in the hallway, watching her. They knew enough to keep their distance, even if they didn't fully understand the tragedy they were witnessing. "What kind of a flower is a Caleb?" Cornelia heard Lilian ask.

Mr. Hale had the good sense to shush Lilian. "Not now!" he whispered. He moved closer, to see if he could comfort Cornelia.

Cornelia picked Caleb up and cradled him in her hands. "I knew this would happen," she said, on the verge of tears. "That cat hates me!"

If only it were just about the cat, Cornelia thought, and not about my one true love. Caleb, please be okay. . . .

She felt her father's strong hands on her shoulders. "There, there!" He soothed her. "Your friend Will gave him to you, didn't she?"

Mentioning Will's name made Cornelia start to think about all that she and her friends had been through over the last few weeks. The feelings she'd kept pent up for weeks were out in the open now, and she was crying the way she hadn't cried since Caleb had been transformed. "I hate her! I hate her!" Cornelia cried.

But she didn't hate Will. She didn't even hate Napoleon. She just hated being separated from Caleb and, more than anything, she hated this awful feeling of being alone. She had once been part of a magical Power of Five. Now, she was quickly learning how lonely and powerless it felt to be by herself.

Cornelia could tell that her dad was mystified at her outburst, but he held her in a tight and loving hug.

Her mother wanted to help ease her pain, too. Cornelia could tell by the way she was looking at her. A moment later, her mother disappeared. When, soon after, she came back into the bedroom, it was to present Cornelia with a beautiful crystal vase. "Look on the bright side, Cornelia," she said. "Now you have the chance to put your flower in something more suitable!"

Cornelia looked up at her mom and gave her a weak smile. The vase was made of beautiful blue crystal. She reached for the vase and gently placed her beloved flower in the water.

At least Caleb is still safe, she thought, stroking the petals and placing the vase on her desk. If only I knew for how long.

EIGHT

Will felt trapped in the front seat of her mother's red car. She was desperately trying to keep her story straight, but under her mother's relentless questioning it was difficult. Her mom was beyond furious, and she was confused by the chaos the girls' visit had caused at her office. Now she wouldn't stop asking questions. Mrs. Vandom was determined to get to the bottom of what had happened at the Simultech offices— and to find out whether her daughter had had something to do with the strange explosion.

Even now, after dropping Hay Lin off at home, her mother was still fuming, and would not change the subject.

"Disappearing like that!" her mother said huffily. "That was foolish, Will."

When her mom was really mad about something, she went on and on about it until it drove Will nearly crazy. Will watched the scenery as they sped to the other side of town, where Irma lived. The tension in the car was mounting, and Will felt as if she had to hold her breath.

"Will, what on earth were you thinking?" Mrs. Vandom asked for what felt like the fiftieth time.

"We were just taking a look around, Mom," Will answered, trying to keep her voice from shaking.

From the backseat, Irma corroborated her story: "And then, when the alarm went off, we ran to the lobby."

Will had to hand it to Irma. Sometimes she was a smooth liar.

"And anyway, there wasn't even a fire, so there is really nothing to worry about," Will pointed out.

That argument didn't work on her mom.

"But there could have been, Will!" her mother said, scolding her. "I'm still shaking! I was so terrified."

There she goes again, Will thought. Always

dwelling on the worst-case scenario.

Ever since her parents had split up, Will's mom had been overprotective to the max. And the funny thing was that even her mom couldn't have dreamt up the thing that had *really* happened at Simultech.

Mrs. Vandom was silent for a moment. Just when Will dared to breathe a sigh of relief, though, she was back at it. "Maybe you didn't hear, but thieves got into Levin Bishop's office, and . . ."

Will couldn't stand to hear any more. And it seemed that Irma couldn't, either. As they waited for a red light to turn green, Irma suddenly had an urge to get out of the car. And fast.

"Um, I think I'll get out here," Irma said. "My house isn't too far away!"

Yeah, right, Irma, Will thought. We're nowhere near your house!

Mrs. Vandom raised an eyebrow and gave Irma a look in the rearview mirror. "Are you sure, Irma?" she asked.

Will tried to catch her friend's eye, but Irma was already opening the door and climbing out.

When she was safely out of the car, Irma leaned in toward Mrs. Vandom's rolled-down window and offered a fumbling explanation. "I don't want to make you drive any further than you have. You already drove Taranee and Hay Lin home."

Mrs. Vandom shrugged and smiled.

"Speaking of which," Irma said to Will, "we were all going to meet up later on. Are you coming, Will?"

Will winked when she was sure her mom wasn't looking. "Of course! We've got to talk about . . . um . . . about . . . that stuff, right?"

"Sorry, Irma," Mrs. Vandom interrupted. "But Will and I have to have a talk tonight. She'll have to meet up with you another time."

"Okay," Irma said, with a dramatic pause.

Will noticed that her friend seemed worried. There was no way the Guardians could miss meeting up later. There was a blue blob roaming around Heatherfield!

"No big deal," Irma said, as casually as she could. "So, Will, I'll call you, okay?"

All Will could do was nod. She hoped that Irma knew that she would try to get away as soon as she could. The girls had to make a plan—together.

As the car left the curb, Will heard Irma

mutter, "Poor Will! I bet she's going to get told off big-time."

Unfortunately, Will was thinking the same thing.

The car was very quiet after Irma left—for most of the ride, Irma's constant chatter had kept the atmosphere almost bearable. To distract herself, Will plotted what she'd do when she got home to avoid her mother's wrath. Her mom couldn't very well fight with Will if Will were in the shower. But how long could she reasonably stay in there? And then, after that, she could claim to have a lot of homework that needed doing.

At that moment, Will just wanted to forget everything that had happened during the afternoon. She reached for the radio, ready to switch on her favorite station, but suddenly she just had to break the ice. She couldn't take the silence anymore.

"Mom," Will said. "If you're mad at me because I went to see you at the office, I . . ."

Mrs. Vandom interrupted in her most serious tone. "Let me talk, because I am only going to say this once."

Will braced herself for the worst. She was

grounded. Her allowance was being reduced to nothing. She couldn't use her cell phone for a month. Who knew what her mom would dream up for her punishment?

Mrs. Vandom stared at the road as she continued. "I want it to be perfectly clear that this time there's no turning back. Whether you like it or not, I'm not changing my mind again, especially since you're the one who wanted it this way. . . ."

What was her mom talking about? It took Will a moment to process her mother's words.

"Wait! Hang on!" Will said. "It was me who wanted what?"

The car slowed down and then stopped for a red light. Mrs. Vandom directed her full attention toward Will. "Levin Bishop will do me the favor of not putting my request through for a transfer. Got it?"

"What?" Will shrieked happily. She couldn't believe it. After all the trouble they'd gone to—and gotten into—things were actually working out as she'd hoped!

As the car lurched forward, Will's high-pitched yowl caused her mom to tap on the brakes a little too hard, and the car's tires went *skeeek* against the road. Throwing her arms around her mom, Will forgot that they were in a moving car. She didn't care about their safety at all. They were staying in Heatherfield!

"Hey! Go easy on the hugs!" cried Mrs. Vandom. "I'm still mad at you!"

But Will knew her mom well enough to know that she was actually happy beneath her cool exterior. She wasn't *always* so bad. . . .

After hearing her mother's news, Will immediately abandoned her plans for a long shower. She forgot all about her homework, too. Instead, she called for a pizza—she and her mom had to celebrate!

Before the pizza party started, Will went in to her room to quickly check her e-mail. "Hello, George!" Will said as she flicked the switch on her computer.

"What can I do for you today?" George replied, coming to life.

One of the strangest of Will's magic powers was her ability to talk to electrical appliances. All of her appliances had names—and personalities. It made checking her answering machine seem more like checking in with a friend.

Will had hoped to find a message from

Cornelia, but no message light was blinking. She longed for Cornelia to be a part of the group again. All five of them had to stick together. It was the only way they'd get to the bottom of this business, with their powers coming and going the way they were. And if it meant that they had to do an intervention with Cornelia, well, Will would have to figure something out. Looking around her room, Will's eyes fell upon a magazine. It was too bad the teen magazines didn't offer advice on what to do when your friend was obsessed with a flower, Will thought wryly.

In the stillness of her room, Will turned her thoughts to earlier in the day. She recalled the giant blob of energy staring at her from the hole in Mr. Bishop's wall. The way it had shifted shape and taken on each of her friends' faces, the way it had jumped out the window and escaped into town, made Will shudder. She had no idea what the blob was, but she had a bad feeling about it.

When the doorbell rang, Will made a conscious effort to push the problem of the blob out of her mind. Will beamed at the delivery guy, then danced toward the table with the pizza. "Mega-super-extra-large pizza! Now, this is what I call a Not-Moving party!" she said, grinning giddily at her mom.

Mrs. Vandom smiled and put her hands over her ears. "Fantastic!" she shouted. "Could you turn the music down? I can't hear the phone!"

So she's back to her usual self, Will thought as she took her first bite of the warm, delicious pizza.

As Will ate her slice of pizza, she thought about the big news bomb her mom had dropped. Will and her mom had had their ups and downs since they'd moved to Heatherfield. It hadn't been easy to build a new life after they'd left Fadden Hills. But they'd made a good start, and they weren't going to give up now. The same was true for her friends, Will realized. They'd only just started to find out what their powers were all about. And they couldn't let them go without a fight.

NINE

As Irma walked home, she felt relieved to be away from Mrs. Vandom's questions. She didn't care if she had to walk ten miles back to her house. There was nothing worse than being present during a fight between one's friend and her mother. Irma was glad to have escaped.

But Will's problem hadn't been solved. The girls had not gotten the letter out of Mr. Bishop's office, to make sure that Will's mom wouldn't be able to relocate. What would W.I.T.C.H. be like without Will? More important, would there be a W.I.T.C.H. at all? Irma didn't even want to think about that. Right now it seemed the girls' powers worked only when Will wove them together using the Heart of Candracar.

Without Will, they didn't seem to be able to use their powers at all. And it looked as though they were going to need all the power they could get, Irma thought. As soon as they managed to find that blob of transforming energy that had disappeared from Simultech, they were going to have to come up with a pretty powerful plan and some powerful magic.

Irma finally reached her house and unlocked the front door. As soon as she put the key in, she realized that there were people talking in the living room. She quietly walked through the door and took her jacket off; her spy skills were already in high gear. She leaned closer to the door so she could try to hear the voices more clearly.

"So, you're really sure?" her father was saying to someone.

"The forensic analysis left no room for doubt," a man replied.

Quickly, Irma stuck her head into the room to get a glimpse of who was talking. Seated on the red couch by the window was the dynamic duo from Interpol: Agents Medina and McTiennan!

What are the agents in charge of Elyon's

investigation doing here? Irma wondered.

There had been plenty of close calls with these two agents, who had been busy snooping around the Browns' home after the family disappeared. No one would have suspected that a portal to another world was in their basement or that quiet Elyon Brown was the queen of Meridian!

No, Irma mused, no one would have thought that Elyon's parents were actually part of the rebel forces in Meridian and changed their very appearance to fit in unsuspected in Heatherfield. Of course, they had to. Their natural blue hair and green skin would have been a definite giveaway, showing that they weren't from around here! But they had a very important role to play. They were protecting the Light of Meridian—Elyon—from her evil brother, Phobos.

Irma slid back away from the living-room door into the front hall. She didn't want to risk being noticed. A few times the agents had questioned her and her friends, and she didn't want to get grilled by Agent Medina or Agent McTiennan now. Plus, Sergeant Lair, aka her dad, would not have been pleased to find his daughter spying on him and his associates.

Then again, lingering in the front hall for a moment wasn't exactly a crime, Irma reasoned. Once again, she leaned in closer to the living-room door to hear more. While she didn't want to talk to the agents, she certainly wanted to hear what they were saying!

"Not to mention the documents registered with the city council," she heard McTiennan say.

"The ones found at the Brown home turned out to be false as well," Medina exclaimed. "Our boss is convinced that Elyon and her parents were illegal aliens!"

Out in the hall, Irma put her hand on her mouth to suppress a giggle. They aren't too far off, she thought, since Elyon's family comes from another world. Score one for the Interpol agents!

"The truth is, our boss wants us to work on another case. . . ." said Medina.

McTiennan interrupted her. "In any event, from now on the whole thing's going to be handled by the immigration authorities," he said rather sternly. "Medina and I are going to clear out once and for all, and . . ."

That meant, Irma realized, that Medina and McTiennan wouldn't be poking around Elyon's house anymore! They would never find the portal! This was great news. The secret of the Brown's house was one less thing for Irma and her friends to have to worry about. At least that secret would be safe. The whole Elyon episode was over, thought Irma.

"Wow!" she said.

Oops!

Irma was so excited about this new development that she'd forgotten to stay quiet. She'd given herself away.

Hearing his daughter's exclamation, Sergeant Lair darted out into the hall and grabbed her by the elbow.

Her dad didn't seem angry so much as confused. "Irma!" he cried. "What are you doing out here? And what's that happy look on your face all about?"

Irma was mortified and, for once, at a total loss for words. "No, no, no, Dad!" she said as she tried to think of some explanation. "I was just . . . just saying hi!" Irma waved into the living room wildly. "How's it going, folks?" she asked, with fake enthusiasm, as if she were the chairperson of some Heatherfield welcoming committee.

As usual, Medina didn't even crack a smile. "Fine, thanks," she replied. "Even if your behavior is a little strange . . . since you already said hello to us!"

What's going on here? Irma thought.

"Huh? Who, me?" she said. There was no way she have would forgotten whether she'd said hello to those two. She had been super-careful not to say a word in the hallway so that she wouldn't be heard.

Irma's dad regarded Irma with utter bewilderment. "Of course!" he said. "You came in through the front door and grunted in this direction, just a moment ago!"

"G—grunted, huh?" Irma stammered. "And then where did I go?"

She didn't care if she sounded insane. She really had to know. After the experience in Simultech, this was not good news. What if the mystery blob was walking around with her face on? What other trouble had it caused? Suddenly, Irma was in full panic mode.

"To your room!" her dad said firmly. "And that's where I'd advise you to go right now, smart aleck!" Her dad pointed to the staircase, in case she'd missed his point.

Irma waved awkwardly at the agents. "Um . . . right, sure!" she cried. "See you around, then!"

Taking two steps at a time, Irma raced up the stairs to her room.

Irma had made astral drops in the past; that was clearly not what was happening this time. Making an astral drop was something that she did by herself—and much too often, if you asked any of her friends. Those astral drops came in handy when the group had to go to fight evil in Meridian. With the astral drops around, no one in Heatherfield missed their presence. But this time, Irma had had nothing to do with the clone!

Irma clenched and unclenched her fists nervously, then started to open her bedroom door. Only one burning question was in her head. Who or what was in there?

Gathering up her courage, she pushed the door open so that whoever was in there would know that the real Irma had arrived. And she was going to make her presence known.

At first glance, everything seemed normal.

Her pink curtains were slightly closed, just as she had left them earlier in the morning. She'd waked up late and not been able to bear the bright sunlight as she jumped into her clothes. Her desk, in the corner of the room, had a couple of books placed neatly on top of it, with a week's worth of French homework stuffed inside.

Above the desk, her favorite pictures were still taped to the wall; a picture of Karmilla, otherwise known as the best singer in the whole world, and some other photos that she'd ripped out of magazines lined the walls.

So far, so good, Irma thought as she surveyed the room. Then her eyes traveled up to the ceiling. Uh-oh! Not so good after all!

Wedged into one of the corners, poised like a spider, was her double! This other Irma looked exactly like the real one, right down to her green tank top and blue skirt, her brown, wavy hair, even her cool new orange flip-flops. And crazier still, the impostor looked as surprised to see Irma as Irma was to see her!

Even though Irma had plenty of experience with astral drops, this situation was way freakier than any she'd been through. At least when it came to her astral drop she had used her own magic to clone herself. This was a different story altogether. Who knew what this creature posing as Irma might do? The impostor could, evidently, climb walls and generally move in ways a regular person couldn't. What other powers did it have?

Irma's mind was in overdrive. Clearly, the blob from Simultech had found its way here and had morphed into a replica of Irma's body. She had to act quickly. Her dad and the agents were right downstairs!

"Well, Mr. Runny Face!" she announced to the creature. "It's you, isn't it? That blob from Simultech?"

The thing didn't answer, which Irma decided to take as a good sign.

Good, I got your attention, Irma thought.

The creature changed its position on the wall, giving the impression it might leap down at any second.

"You've changed your clothes," Irma said to the Irma-poser. "And they're in full color this time!"

She had to smirk a little at her own joke. The blob was definitely showing better taste wearing an exact replica of her outfit than it had dressed in its blue blob color.

As Irma watched the impostor, she noticed that it was clutching a photograph in its hand.

What is that a photograph of? Irma wondered.

The impostor was now dangerously close to the open window. It made a quick lurch, but Irma was faster. She shut the window in one fast move, before the creature could get outside and run away . . . again.

"Oh, no, you don't!" she cried. "Before you jump out the window again, you've got a lot of explaining to do!"

Even though Irma's powers were on the fritz, she still had the ability to outsmart a blue blob. Not only was she a Guardian of the Veil, she was a sergeant's daughter! She knew how to handle an interrogation—she'd learned from a master. But her courage failed her when she caught a closer glimpse of the photograph the creature was clutching.

"What are you doing with that photo of Cornelia?" Irma demanded. She glared angrily at the creature, who must have stolen the picture from her desk. Irma's imitator was waving the photograph around like a trophy.

Then the creature began to morph again, right before Irma's eyes! Where Irma's face had been two seconds before, there was now just a blue blob. Just as the blob had shifted shapes in Mr. Bishop's office, it now began to change into a being that looked exactly like Cornelia.

How could this beast just morph into Cornelia by using a photograph? thought Irma. What sort of creature was this? Irma had a feeling that the situation was getting more dire by the minute. Now the creature could just look at a photograph and morph. And just when she thought things couldn't get any worse, the door to her bedroom flew open to reveal Agent Medina standing in the doorway.

"Excuse me, Irma," she said in her quiet way. "I wanted to say good-bye, and . . ."

Agent Medina's jaw dropped when she saw the blob huddling in the corner of the ceiling. It had Irma's body with Cornelia's face, but it was in the middle of morphing its face back into Irma's. As Agent Medina watched in disbelief, the creature took on the look of a pile of quivering blue gelatin. Irma stood with her back to the window, her arms spread out parallel to the sill; she was trying to look casual. It didn't matter, though. Agent Medina's eyes were riveted on the blob.

She must be really freaking out, Irma thought as she watched the agent rub her eyes in disbelief. I'm sure she doesn't see this sort of thing every day.

The blob had finished shifting back into its Irma form. Once again there were two Irmas in the room. One stood near the window, and one hovered in the air. Agent Medina pushed her glasses up to the top of her head. She rubbed her eyes more vigorously. "Th—that's impossible!" she said to herself "I—"

Irma saw that she had to do something *fast*. She threw open her window again with a clunk. The blob hopped off the ceiling and jumped through the open window.

She knew it was dangerous to let the creature out to roam the streets of Heatherfield, but she also knew that Agent Medina was not the ideal person to discover the truth of the creature's appearance. Under the circumstances, she had no choice but to let the thing go.

Maybe this overworked agent will think she needs to get a stronger prescription for her glasses, Irma thought hopefully as she watched the woman massage her temples and then put her glasses back up on her forehead.

Or maybe, as Irma's dad had often said about Medina, she'd think work was getting to her and that she needed a vacation.

Irma held her position by the window. She didn't breathe. She didn't dare move. Her face was frozen in a smile. She tried to look non-chalant.

Agent Medina turned away and continued to rub her eyes. By the time she put her glasses back on and turned to face Irma, the blob had disappeared. Now Medina was staring directly at Irma.

"I—I think I need to rest," the agent stammered. She straightened her jacket and smoothed her hair. Then she shook her head as she gave the room one more look. "Excuse me, but I really have to be going!"

With a small wave, she left, closing the door behind her.

Irma leaned against the window and shut her eyes. She let out a big sigh of relief. That had been way too close. But she couldn't rest for long, there was too much to do. If only she had had the power to stop the crazy creature, she thought. She had to focus. And she had to warn the others. There was no telling what this shape-shifter was capable of—and it had Cornelia's picture!

TEN

Tibor stood at attention next to the Oracle in the Temple of Candracar. The normally peaceful and tranquil place was now tense and full of anxiety as news of the activities of the Altermere traveled through the crowd. Watching the most recent episode at Irma's house in the reflecting pool, Tibor was not surprised.

The Oracle was infinitely patient. But Tibor did not share that quality. Though he was the Oracle's most trusted adviser, he was growing increasingly nervous and frustrated at the situation. As he watched the scene unfolding in Irma's bedroom, Tibor began to pace and to stroke his long white beard nervously.

"The Altermere is free!" Tibor exclaimed when Irma opened the window. "The Guardian has let it escape!"

Nodding, the Oracle acknowledged that what Tibor had said was true. He took a deep breath and then turned to Tibor to explain. "She had no choice," he said. "You forget that it also holds her power."

Tibor knew that the Altermere contained some of Irma's power and that Irma did not have the ability to stop the creature. But how could the Oracle have let this tragedy happen? The Oracle must have been aware of the damage the Altermere could cause in Heatherfield. He must have had a plan. Tibor had never doubted the Oracle's choices.

The Oracle turned away from the reflecting pool and strode into the Aura Hall. Tibor quickly followed. He watched as the Oracle's shoulders slumped in dismay when he saw what had become of the Aurameres. Since Luba had interfered, the Aurameres were no longer contained in a peaceful sphere but were in disarray.

What a tragedy this was, Tibor thought sadly. And to have it happen right after the Guardians successfully completed their first task makes it all the more tragic.

Though Luba was quick to point out the faults of the young Guardians, Tibor had had faith in the Oracle's decision to appoint the girls as the Chosen Ones. In addition, the girls had successfully performed their earlier tasks of closing the portals and restoring the throne of Meridian to its rightful heir.

A single Auramere colored bright green darted past Tibor's head as he walked into the Aura Hall. Tibor knew that it was Cornelia's Auramere. The green spark reflected the power of the earth and was therefore representative of Cornelia. There was also a large sphere swirling in the hall made up of four colors that was the "Altermere's Auramere."

What a dangerous race, thought Tibor. The big sphere is seeking the green Auramere at the same time the Altermere is seeking Cornelia!

The searching Auramere flew wildly toward the ceiling and then zoomed past the Oracle and Tibor straight toward the floor. There seemed to be no way to predict its path.

"Observe, Tibor!" the Oracle said. "What is happening on the earth is reflected here in the Aura Hall!" As the green Auramere flew by them once again, the Oracle pointed to it. "The single Auramere formed by the union of the four powers is out of control. It wants to absorb Cornelia's Auramere as well—but it can't quite find it!"

Tibor nodded. Now he was beginning to understand the connection between events at Irma's house and those there in Candracar.

"At this very moment, the same thing is happening in Heatherfield!" The Oracle exclaimed.

Uneasily, Tibor observed the Auramere careening around the Hall. He stroked his beard as he often did when he was thinking. The creature that was in Irma's room was an Altermere, created when the powers of the Guardians had all become fused together. All the powers were joined together except the power over earth. And now, that Altermere would stop at nothing to absorb the fifth Guardian's power.

"I see!" Tibor cried. "In some way, the Altermere has perceived Irma's memories, and now it knows whom to go after." Tibor was suddenly struck by a horrible thought. The Altermere was gaining strength, and now that it had some of Irma's memories from which to gather information, the situation could only get worse. "It went to Irma's house," Tibor said, "convinced it could track down Cornelia." He hoped that the Oracle would offer some assurance. But as he looked up at his leader, he saw that the Oracle's usually serene face held an expression of grave concern.

"Yes!" the Oracle confirmed. "I'm afraid so."

The Altermere is running loose through Heatherfield at this very moment, Tibor thought. And it's intent on finding Cornelia and obtaining her power. There was no silver lining to this situation, Tibor knew. But the Altermere still had to find Cornelia.

"It acts on instinct," the Oracle explained. "It doesn't know where to find the holder of the powers of the earth! To do so, it will seek out a guide."

It was terrible to consider a powerful Altermere roaming freely in the streets of Heatherfield. There was still some time, however, before the Altermere would have its way. And, Tibor thought, one should never underestimate the Guardians.

ELEVEN

Taranee stood on the street corner where she, Irma, and Hay Lin had arranged to meet. The three of them had made the plan immediately after Irma's urgent phone call. This was definitely an emergency.

It was a cloudy gray afternoon, and seagulls circled ominously above the trees. Would anybody else have found the gulls ominous? Taranee wondered. Maybe not. But their eerie squawking suited her mood. Things did not look good, and it didn't help that the two of the five Guardians who weren't there were incommunicado.

Tapping her foot on the pavement, Taranee tried not to be impatient. She looked over at Hay Lin, who was in a phone booth, trying to reach Cornelia.

If only Cornelia hadn't been so adamant about wanting to be left alone, Taranee thought. Taranee wanted to talk to her friend and to help her.

Hay Lin came out of the phone booth, shaking her head. "No luck," she said. "Cornelia isn't answering."

These days, Cornelia is *always* home, Taranee thought. She never leaves her room— or her flower.

"I bet she took it off the hook so she wouldn't have to talk to anyone," Hay Lin said.

Knowing that Cornelia had her own phone line in her room, that seemed very likely, Taranee thought.

"And I still can't get ahold of Will!" Hay Lin exclaimed.

Taranee detected some alarm in Hay Lin's voice. At least she feels it, too, Taranee thought. Where has everybody gone? What are we supposed to do now? What happened to the Power of Five?

Irma was the only one who had any new information. She'd been the last to see Will, and she described to the others what had happened in the car after they had been dropped off.

"Her mom was totally furious with her," Irma told them. "I wouldn't want to be in her shoes right now!"

Will's fighting with her mom about what happened at Simultech is not a good development, Taranee reflected. Things really have spiraled out of control. If only our powers were stronger and we were more in control. We used to work better when we were a team, a team of five. Now, knowing that Will and her mom have had a big fight, it seems likely that our mission this morning was a total wash. It's beginning to look as if Will might be leaving Heatherfield.

Taranee considered the possibility. Will's leaving was a horrible thing to think about. Taranee knew that she had to remain strong and focused. Even though her powers were at an all-time low, she still was a Chosen One. And right now, there was a dangerous creature on the prowl looking for Cornelia.

A plan suddenly popped into Taranee's head. She knew it might be dangerous. But what other choice did they have?

"It looks like we'll have to go see Cornelia without Will," Taranee said. "We at least have to warn her."

"Yes," Hay Lin agreed. "Since that crazy blob thing took on her appearance, it might be looking for her!"

Taranee smiled at Hay Lin. She was glad that at least Hay Lin was on the same wavelength. Looking at Irma, though, she wasn't sure what the water guru was thinking. Irma had her arms crossed behind her head and her eyes closed.

How could she be so calm? Taranee wondered as she watched Irma. She's the one who witnessed the blob morphing into Cornelia. She ought to know how dire this situation is getting.

"Oh, come on," Irma finally said, exhaling loudly. "Last time, it was Frost who was looking for her. Now it's just some pudding-faced chameleon!"

Taranee rolled her eyes as she looked at Hay Lin. Frost the Hunter had been one of Prince Phobos's men. Frost had came to Heatherfield seeking revenge for what the Guardians had done in Meridian. But, Taranee thought, Irma was wrong. He hadn't just been searching for Cornelia—he'd been searching for all of the girls. Forever the drama queen, Irma never liked being outshone . . . even if it was in being hunted down by some otherworldly creep!

"I have to say," Irma continued. "Cornelia's got way too many boyfriends from other worlds!"

Taranee decided there wasn't any more time for arguing with Irma. Rather than responding to her wisecrack about Cornelia's history of otherworldly dates, Taranee stalked off in the direction of Cornelia's house. Someone has got to lead here, she thought. To her relief, Hay Lin and even Irma followed her right away.

"Well, think about it," Taranee said. "Heatherfield's big. Why did that thing go straight to Irma's house?" She looked at her friends. "It knows who we are!" she told Hay Lin and Irma as they walked on. "And it wants something from us."

Taranee quickened her pace. She tried not to run—she didn't want people on the street to gawk at her or the other two crazed teenagers running with her through the streets. But she felt like running. She had to get to Cornelia.

They came to an intersection. Rather than turning and crossing the street toward Cornelia's building, though, Irma kept on walking in the same direction as before, heading away from Cornelia's.

"Where are you going?" Taranee said. "You know the way!"

Irma signaled to the other girls. "Do you guys get the sense we're being followed?" she whispered.

Taranee scanned the area as quickly as she could. She didn't see a thing.

"I feel it, too, Irma," Hay Lin said. "Even though I haven't seen anyone near us. I can't explain it, but I know what you mean."

Taranee shook her head. "We need to get to Cornelia's," she said firmly. "Let's just try to get there before anyone else!"

We can't abandon our plan now, Taranee thought. Even if we are being followed. . . .

The girls broke into a full sprint and ran until they arrived at Cornelia's building. By then they were out of breath and gasping for air.

"Here we are!" said Irma, panting. "Let's hope she doesn't tell us to get lost!"

"We all know she's got her tough side,"

Taranee commented. "But there's no reason for her to be that way now. Especially after we explain why we're here."

"The fact is," Hay Lin added, "we probably should have come to see her a long time ago."

In the posh lobby of the high-rise apartment building, Irma buzzed Cornelia's apartment. Taranee braced herself for rejection, in spite of what she'd just said to her friends. She knew that Cornelia had been impossible lately. It might be hard to get through to her, but they had to warn her that she was in danger.

When Cornelia's voice came over the speaker, Irma pressed the button and spoke into the box. "Hi, Corny!" she yelled, using her nickname for Cornelia. "It's us! We have to talk!"

To the surprise of all of them, Cornelia sounded upbeat. "Fantastic!" she practically cheered. "Top floor! But you remember the way, don't you?"

Irma gave Taranee and Hay Lin a look of disbelief.

Something had changed, Taranee thought. Cornelia seemed ready to talk to them for the first time since they'd returned from Meridian.

And it was not a moment too soon!

"Hear how happy she sounds?" Taranee exclaimed. "I can't wait to tell Will!"

When the elevator's doors opened, Hay Lin was lagging behind in the lobby.

"Want to hurry up, Hay Lin?" Taranee called out. "The elevator won't wait!"

Hay Lin was busy writing on her hand with her blue pen. "I was just jotting down Cornelia's exact words," she explained as she slipped into the elevator.

After glancing at Hay Lin's hands, Irma scowled at her friend. "Will you stop scribbling on your hands? You're going to poison yourself someday!"

Normally Hay Lin would have laughed off a comment like that, but, since the tension between the girls was at an all-time high, Taranee was curious to see what Hay Lin would do. Breezy, carefree Hay Lin seemed to let the comment roll off her back.

Just as the elevator doors were about to close, Taranee noticed someone running toward the nearby stairwell. And that someone looked very familiar!

"Hey, look!" she shouted, just as the doors

of the elevator shut. "That girl running up the stairs . . . that can't be Will, can it?"

The thought sent a shiver down Taranee's spine. She knew that Will was at home with her mother. She also knew that the blob was able to shift shape quickly; it had morphed into Will once before. If this creature was posing as Will, and if it got to Cornelia's apartment before they did, the result could be disastrous.

Please hurry, Taranee begged silently as she watched the elevator pass each of the floors. We need to reach Cornelia before that impostor does!

TWELVE

Cornelia was thankful for the silence in her apartment. With her parents and Lilian at the movies, the penthouse was quiet and calm. Lilian wasn't running around making noise while she chased Napoleon, and Cornelia's parents weren't watching her with concern in their eyes. Cornelia sighed as she sprawled out on her bed. Finally, I'm alone! she thought.

Cornelia stretched. She felt different today. She had more energy. For days and weeks on end, it had been hard for Cornelia to do so much as leave her room and sit down with her family at the dinner table. Now, though, she felt ready for something.

I went into hibernation just the way bears do, she mused. My dad was definitely right about my being like that. I wonder if bears ever long for the world outside during their long winter naps.

Reaching far above her head, Cornelia stretched and yawned. She did miss her regular routine. For the first time in a long time, she admitted to herself how much she missed being a part of the world beyond her bedroom.

At Sheffield Institute, she was a true Infielder; she knew everyone, and everyone knew her. Cornelia's flair for style and her cool confidence were easy to spot in the hallways. And, Cornelia realized, she missed her friends.

She rolled over onto her stomach and looked at the phone next to her bed. She couldn't remember the last time she'd telephoned someone or the last time she'd received a call, for that matter.

Well, she thought, I guess that it's time to reestablish contact with the outside world.

Grabbing the phone, Cornelia placed the receiver back on its base. You can ring now, phone, she instructed it silently.

With lots of new energy pulsing through her, Cornelia couldn't bear to lie around.

I don't know what's gotten into me, she

thought. It's as if I were waking up from a bad dream.

Cornelia flipped over, propped herself up on her elbows, and looked around. She saw her room in a brand-new light, just as if she'd been a bear waking up from a long, cold winter's sleep.

She looked at her stuffed animals, sitting in a line against her pillow. One of them was a bunny rabbit that had been in her crib when she was a baby. Reaching out, she began to pet its ears. It made her feel like a little girl again. She regarded her ice skates, hanging on the wall near her bed. Cornelia loved to skate, but it seemed a lifetime since she had glided over the ice without a care in the world.

And finally, of course, there was Caleb. His new home was the expensive antique vase her mother had given her.

Cornelia thought back to the awful moment that afternoon when Napoleon had smashed Caleb's dish. When her mother handed her the beautiful vase to use instead, Cornelia had felt like throwing it back in her face. The point wasn't that the dish was broken. The point was that Cornelia had allowed it to fall and break.

Caleb's life was so fragile, so dependent on her constant care. Cornelia was angry with herself for being negligent. She blamed herself for leaving the door open. She even blamed herself for what the cat had done . . . though she had to share the blame for that one. Napoleon really was an awful cat. Cornelia wished she had never allowed him into the house.

But just then, she wasn't in the mood to dwell on the negatives. She didn't need to sulk about things she couldn't control. For once, she was ready to look on the bright side.

I was kind of unfair to Mom, Cornelia thought. That antique vase is probably very valuable. I should have acted more grateful when she gave it to me.

It made Cornelia deeply happy to think of her precious Caleb's dwelling in an expensive work of art. It was what he deserved.

The vase is worthy of the flower it holds, Cornelia thought. Speaking of which . . . I should probably give Caleb a bit of fresh air.

Cornelia sprang up from her bed filled with purpose. She drew back her pink curtains and stepped outside onto a narrow balcony bathed in sunlight. She looked out over peaceful

Heatherfield. Then she closed her eyes and relished the feeling of the cool breeze ruffling her long blond hair. Cornelia couldn't remember the last time she had felt so contented.

Buzzzzzzzz! Buzzzzzzzz!

The intercom was sounding.

Who could that be? Cornelia wondered.

She wandered over to the box in the hallway by the front door. Yesterday Cornelia would have ignored the intrusion and hid out in her room. But today she figured she had nothing to lose by seeing who was there.

"Yes?" she said brightly into the intercom.

"Hi, Corny! It's us! We have to talk!"

Cornelia was shocked to see Irma's image in the intercom's video monitor. She was so happy, in fact, that she wasn't even mad that Irma had used her silly nickname for her.

If I were in her shoes, Cornelia thought, I would have given up on me by now.

It was a relief to find that her friends were determined to stay in touch! And it wasn't only Irma who was downstairs. . . . Hay Lin and Taranee were there, too.

She buzzed them in with great anticipation. She had so much to talk to them about!

Cornelia flung open the apartment door and looked at the elevator directly across the hall. She could see that the elevator was just leaving her floor to go down. . . . It would be a few minutes till the girls got upstairs.

That elevator is *so-o-o* slow, Cornelia thought. Nothing can go fast enough for me right now! I feel so full of energy! Yes! I really feel like talking to the girls. And I have the house all to myself, too!

Now Cornelia could see the elevator light up indicating that it was in the lobby. She imagined her friends boarding, the doors closing, and the three of them drawing closer to her apartment.

"Meeeeow!" wailed Napoleon, from somewhere inside the apartment.

Cornelia turned around. "Be quiet, you silly cat!" Cornelia shouted.

She ran back into the apartment to see what kind of mischief the cat was getting into.

As she ran through the apartment, Cornelia could hear the cat meowing. She remembered that her bedroom door was closed. He wouldn't be able to do any more damage this time.

But . . . the sounds were coming from her

room. Then she realized something awful. She'd left the window to her balcony open.

Oh, no! The cat could have gotten into my room from the outside! she thought.

"You mean old cat!" Cornelia called to him as she turned her doorknob. "Closing my door wasn't enough to stop you, huh?"

She flung open the door. "Don't you dare touch . . ."

But Napoleon wasn't touching anything. In fact, he was chasing something!

A huge black crow was hovering over Caleb's vase, its talons extended. "Caw! Caw! Caw!" it cried, and the sound pierced Cornelia's heart. The birds talons were ready to rip into Caleb!

But Napoleon held the bird at bay. "Ffft," he hissed, arching his back. Napoleon lunged at the crow, and, before Cornelia had a moment to collect her thoughts, the bird flew away through her open window. Napoleon didn't quiet down, though. "Meow!" he screeched until the crow was well out of sight. "Meow!"

A crow, thought Cornelia mechanically. It was pecking at the flower!

Cornelia's heart sank. She'd been feeling so

great before . . . *but what if Caleb had been hurt?* With great fear, she drew near his vase to examine his petals. She breathed a huge sigh of relief. Caleb was in one piece!

Upon close examination, however, Cornelia saw small round marks on the petals. She'd seen them earlier in the day, after Napoleon broke the dish, and she'd assumed they had been caused by the accident. Now she thought about it again.

The falling dish didn't cause these marks on the petals, Cornelia thought. Now that I think about it, the window was open this afternoon, too. That crow flew into my room not once, but twice!

"You didn't want to hurt Caleb," Cornelia said to the black cat. "You wanted to protect him!"

Now that Cornelia knew who the real villain was, she had some apologies to make. Napoleon was sitting under the vase, nuzzling the bottom of it and purring. Cornelia picked him up and whirled around the room with him in her arms. She would be eternally grateful to this cat. She would do anything for him!

"Napoleon, you're a wonderful cat!"

Cornelia sang, with tears of relief rolling down her cheeks. She spun around and around with him till they both were dizzy. Things had been dicey there for a moment, but Cornelia's magnificent mood was back. Nothing could get her down now!

Cornelia lifted Napoleon up toward the ceiling and gazed into his brown eyes. Cornelia knew that the two of them hadn't always been friends, but that had changed the moment she saw him fight off the crow. Napoleon was Caleb's protector!

When she saw Will again, she would have to thank her for this most special gift. Cornelia had a feeling she hadn't been properly grateful at the time Will had brought Napoleon to her.

That cat was certainly the best gift Cornelia had ever gotten. He had saved Caleb's life!

Wait until I tell the girls, Cornelia thought happily. With Napoleon snuggling in her arms, Cornelia walked back toward the front of the apartment. She was ready to greet her friends. She had lots to share with them.

Things are going to be different now, she thought. Very different.

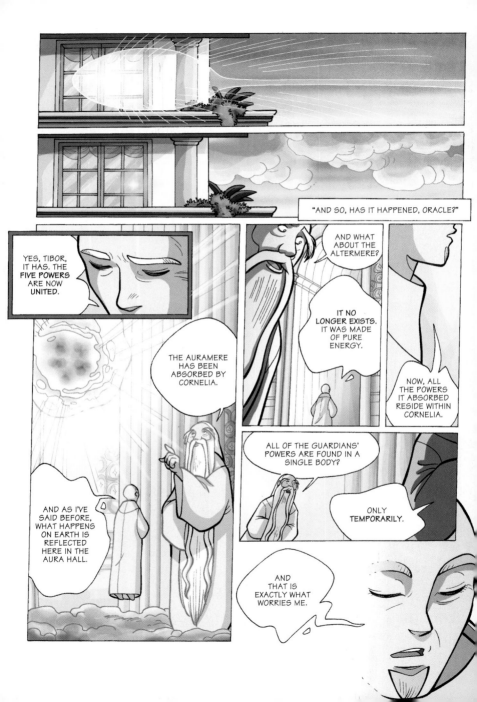

TO BE CONTINUED . . .